Incredible Revelations
of an Earthworm

Copyright © 2024 by Domício Coutinho
Translation copyright © 2024 by Clifford E. Landers
Interview copyright © 2022 by George Salis
Introduction copyright © 2024 by George Salis
Back cover photo courtesy of the Brazilian Endowment for the Arts.

ISBN 979-8-218-34629-4

Tough Poets Press
Arlington, Massachusetts 02476
U.S.A.

www.toughpoets.com

Domício Coutinho
§
Incredible Revelations of an Earthworm

Translated from the Portuguese
by Clifford E. Landers

Introduction and interview
by George Salis

Tough Poets Press
Arlington, Massachusetts

Introduction

"The love that takes us to heaven is the twin of the hatred that casts us into the abyss. In the hands of the two, we never know where we are, and care little about the end."

The worm. A creature unsung at best and unseemly at worst. When remembered at all, it's often used as an insult or invoked as the eater of the dead, memento mori, excepting the term "bookworm," although even that can have a negative connotation, of being at the margins, away from the thick of life. The worm, almost as unjustly reviled as the snake. Yet the worm was a muse of Charles Darwin, a creature that boasts no bones, making it more flexible and sinuous than humans could ever hope to be. Like vultures, they are decomposers, taking on the thankless task of cleaning up the world. Notions of the morbid aside, an abundance of these hermaphrodites is a sign of healthy soil. Still, none of these are reasons why I invariably lean over during walks and pick up with naked fingers the worms marooned on asphalt or concrete, those on the verge of baking alongside their desiccated kin. It's because life deserves to live. This respect for the beings in the web of nature, of which we're but a thread, is something Domício Coutinho possesses in Aesopian spades. It's a respect that can be traced to a wider reverence for creation, including the creation of creation, that first story which has within itself every story, including its own endless permutations: "Those stories and visions convinced me of one thing, that the human mind comes from long-lost eras of history, fragmented, however, like a mirror shattered into a thousand pieces, reflecting the world around it, ever since the first word was uttered." Throughout *Incredible Revelations of an Earthworm*, Coutinho gives us his tinkered and tailored versions of these oldest of tales. According to this novel, worms are creatures of the highest order, including a vermicular character in particular: "She was a noble, her blue blood came from the origins of the world. The first animal to appear on the planet. The chrysalis in which the plants transformed. She descended directly from the first woman, to whom the Great Kyrios said: 'Let there be the earthworm!'"

All these tales exist within one or more frame tales, the first one featuring an observant and thoughtful if at times judgmental man who spends most of his time along the beach, which, we are told, is a place ripe for creative minds: "Beethoven is said to have conceived the Sixth Symphony beside the ocean. Shakespeare wrote *The Tempest* listening to the waves." The beach, a perfect foundation for a novel obsessed with inception, especially considering how water is the stuff of life, or at least of life as we know it, the beach as the bridge between one creation story and that of another, our momentous transition from water into land, when we turned the sea inside out and kept it within ourselves, our bodies, more than half of which is made up of water. We are ocean sacks. About his own creation, the protagonist says, "I knew that the Potter, when He made me, was dead tired, as he left me all twisted and out of place. And his breath was short. Instead of entering through the nostrils, it escaped through the forehead."

As a character, Eve eventually boils down the myth of creation into its dichotomous essence: dark and light. Darkness, being photophobic, engages in a well-nigh nuclear war with its radiant counterpart. This section of primordial fireworks is but the stage for further tales and tidbits. Before and after, we learn why the flamingo stands on one leg all day long, that the movement of the crab delineated Einstein's theory of relativity, why the fishes of the earth lose control at the sight of a worm (hint: it's for reasons lascivious), how Man came from Woman rather than the reverse, and how Neptune invented nepotism. We also learn about vermiphagos kings, the donkey Zeferino who participates in the events at Golgotha, Washington's pact with the Devil, a shark with well-founded misanthropy, the meaning of "skull fights," and more.

Having studied Aristotelian Thomistic theology at the Gregorian University of Rome and later quitting the seminary, it should be expected that Coutinho offers readers religious criticism that focuses mostly on Christianity (although this is a novel that incorporates paganism into its cosmos), both through the protagonist's mouth and the worm's, those incredible revelations as promised by the title: "During all the drama of the Passion, he had not appeared even once, nor said a word during the judgment and the death on the hill between two criminals. Nothing to comfort, nothing to reprehend, nothing. Just as if he didn't want to know about Him. That silence must have been his greatest torment. What father would close his eyes and leave his son alone in the hands of executioners, dying on a cross?" What father, indeed. Another example, this regarding faith, referred to with a feminine pronoun: "She speaks and inspires really anyone, but suddenly abandons her most devout followers and clients, those enraptured ones who bought her enchantments at inflationary prices. Those she treats like a femme fatale who takes pleasure in painting the splendors of the few instants she spends with lovers on earth, deluding them with the promise of sempiternal ecstasy in a golden palace, without to the present day ever having given the tiniest demonstration that such a palace exists." This type of criticism is similar in spirit to Coutinho's first novel, *Duke, the Dog Priest*, which professes against the injunction of celibacy, although that book (my personal favorite) is more Márquezian, with a nested structure more traditionally based in character and an over-arching narrative, while *Incredible Revelations of an Earthworm*'s structure and style is more Voltairean, an expository-heavy novel of ideas and lambastes fueled by fanciful zoology. Still, these books also share a necessary humorous irreverence. Let's not forget that the truest reverence comes with more than a hint of irreverence because to love something you must know it for all it is—the difference between blind faith and something insightful, something truer.

By the novel's end, Coutinho distills stories into two overlapping dichotomies: the stories of Homer and the stories of Moses, the former stories ruled by Gods and the latter by God: "One day Homer said, 'Look, Moses, there are already enough myths for a forest of books.' Moses, less dour that day, agreed: 'You're right, Homer, let's bring everything together and make it just one story. I'll tell it one way, you another, and in the end, we'll choose which is prettier.'" Which is the ugly story and which the pretty, which the dark and which the light? Just ask the crab that walks backward but is really walking forward and he'll tell you that it's all a matter of perspective.

Coda: After I first read Coutinho's wonderful debut novel, *Duke, the Dog Priest*, and wrote about it for my column *Invisible Books*, I tracked him down for an interview, facilitated by his kind son, the historian Charles Coutinho. In that rare interview, Coutinho Senior says, "I long for the day that [*Incredible Revelations of an Earthworm*] will be translated into English." My review-interview project spurred the interest of Clifford E. Landers, the original translator of Coutinho's first novel, who took on the task and helped make a nonagenarian's dream come true. Afterward, in my capacity as volunteer acquisitions specialist, I sent the manuscript to Rick Schober for potential publication at Tough Poets Press. And the rest is a product of yet another creation story.

George Salis

George Salis is the author of the novel *Sea Above, Sun Below*. He's the winner of the Tom La Farge Award for Innovative Writing. He's also the editor of www.TheCollidescope.com, an online publication that celebrates innovative and neglected literature. After nearly a decade, he has almost finished working on a maximalist novel titled *Morphological Echoes*. www.GeorgeSalis.com

Chapter One

That holiday, I came up with the idea of running on the beach. A verdant picturesque panorama of a Caribbean island. Irresistible magic of a May morning. Cool wind, the changing colors of the sea from blue to green to grayish-green. A bright chocolate-green dominated the tropical landscape. What most impressed me were the silvery waves. Fury and gentleness. In a soupçon of the playfulness of impetuous little girls tumbling over each other and throwing themselves onto the rocks. False daughters of Neptune who went away, while they remained, recalling the ancient savage.

A strong wind, wicked as only it could be, lashed my face, my chest, my sides, wrapping itself around my legs, crazy-cool, hindering the run. The daring, impertinent seashore wind.

Still, I shouldn't blame it but rather the fascination of the landscape that took me beyond the point of return. To the place the fishermen called "Hill of the Crosswinds." Driving everything mad when it arrived. Ambling horses free in the countryside suddenly stop, raising and lowering their manes. Twirling lightly, swaying in circles, a weird, garish dance of haunches, as if they were ridden by ne'er-do-well goblins. Suddenly, they leave, flinging themselves into the waves, the rocks, the haughty coconut palms, in every direction, in a veritable fury of the possessed, whistling and howling the tragic song of the mermaids.

It was fascinating. The beach itself suddenly was hidden by the half moon, forming a bay at the foot of a steep decline full of holes. Above, a chorus of scattered coconut trees rustled. Below, gigantic monstrous rocks, misshapen, piled up in the sand. People arriving and sitting down to listen to the chorus of winds lamenting their fate, their sins and curses, which winds have too, according to fishermen. Peaceful and open people, but full of superstition.

Seven horses altogether, it was said, baptized in keeping with their nature and disposition. El Teleu, El Gisel, El Flavô, El Lulu, El Carol, commanded by the sleek and charismatic El Mondeu with his limber and fluttering shimmy, his tail whirling in the air to guide them. A master of the winds never errs a toss. Except the most recent, El Cecil, proud and indomitable, loose and running without reins on the beach.

Rebellious, they cause lightning to flash and thunder to resound on clear nights, creating the storms that rage and shake the earth. Some delighted in disturbing the peaceful dead in their graves and dragging them dancing along the highways, their luminous raiment flapping in the wind. Those were not winds at all but spirits, wandering and moaning deliriously. In the next incarnation, they said, they would become adorable people. Angels of kindness and generosity. No one would be able to recognize them, or even suspect that they were only crosswinds. A bizarre belief of those fishermen, accepted and believed by many even today.

Those stories and visions convinced me of one thing, that the human mind comes from long-lost eras of history, fragmented, however, like a mirror shattered into a thousand pieces, reflecting the world around it, ever since the first word was uttered.

Chapter Two

Soon afterward, I saw a group of what I thought were hippies. I was totally mistaken. Fifteen to eighteen at most, spread out on the shore they sat or stretched out on their backs, their bewildered faces open to the sky. One of them was balanced on one leg, with the other raised the way an alchemist keeps his feet under the table, faithfully honoring a contract signed in blood with witches to guarantee success and fame, but who discovered it wasn't enough and demanded that it also inspire stories to delight the world of today and eras yet to come. And they agreed in exchange for his soul and his mustache. The contract stipulated one leg in the air when writing, at dinner, peeing, or making love. To judge from appearances and what linguists tell us, a great poet from overseas was also thought to have signed a contract with those same witches, or their counterparts. Except that it was his flamingo that kept one leg suspended all day long.

To find out the truth, I searched in vain for those selfsame ladies, who were never at home and didn't even have the courtesy to return my calls. I gave up. I would offer them two legs instead of one, raised at the same time. My mustache, a precious inheritance from my grandparents, and, to boot, the remnants of my white hair, the final oasis in the desert that dominates the landscape. In exchange, I would receive inspiration and art for some modern dialogues which, if no match for Plato's, might at least possess something of the magic that captivated the alchemist.

Cynics say that the witches laughed at me then and still do.

Very well. I'm tired of telling Dona Philó's son not to get involved with those people. The blockhead never listens to me.

The hippies. One rested his hand on his knee. Another, in the static pose of a Watteau clown. Still another, cane in hand, wide-brimmed hat, might be a scientist hunting butterflies.

The presence of such people gathered there struck me as both shocking and all too prosaic. Dressed as they were, not in swimwear but the way you attend a summer concert in Central Park, or a lunatics' picnic. Everyone in black or dark clothing. Men and women, adolescents of both sexes, likable males, adorable females, despite the apparent craziness, attentive and deep into the voices from beyond.

The impression it awoke in me was to suddenly relive the days of Woodstock, which I had visited not so long ago. I recalled the great event of the Sixties when young people rocked the world, shaking traditions into the wind. Victorian America vanished in a cyclone! Goodbye to the discipline of manners, to life, to private or public behavior, to tastes and everything, whether rough, refined, or elitist. Barbaric things residing in each of us were revived. Anyone who didn't board the convoy to Woodstock would miss the train of History or of the millennium. The great "Taking of the Bastille" of ethics and customs occurred in those days.

Young men and women, old men and children, fathers and mothers of families, happily joined the sound of rock and frolic, naked, drunken, hallucinated, divine, in the streets, the forests, the rivers. They were returning to paradise. More than a eucharistic congress of drugs and, yes, of kisses and tongues, in voracious communion: take and eat, this is my body.

Flags of sexual revolution were unfurled. And the society

born from the tie between man and woman yielded to the *homo*, executioners of the contract that demanded recognition and an integral role in the process.

That lack of direction would impact the soul of the Church, take over the pulpits and penetrate cells and convents. Behold apostles of Christ trading the Gospel for Marxist economics and the politics of the masses. Blusterers in the Church began to recast poverty as ignominy, forgetting that poverty was beautiful and holy, the noble flower of the Gospel, embodying a mystique sung and transplanted from the gardens of the Bible. Being poor was chic and, additionally, an easy and comfortable life. Just like wealth, a question of habit, temperament and stoic vocation hidden in the genes of the species. The imagery of the lilies of the field and the birds in the sky, perhaps the most beautiful of many found in the Gospel, has always irresistibly excited the soul of rich and poor alike. But the rich treat it as a lure, a dangerous chimera, a metaphor, or at most an angelic jest, save for the respect owed Him who recounted it. Some went so far as to consider it unfortunate. While it fell to the poor to transform it into a system of life. Dreaming. How lovely it is to dream of the purple lilies with which the Heavenly Father will someday adorn us! Without our needing to sweat to attain them. Enough to pray infinite chaplets and litanies, dreaming of taking the life of pleasure from the rich, maligning them, and consigning them to the place they deserve in the Gehennas. Crossing their arms, their spirit legs in the symbolic pose of new Christian Buddhas. With a small prayer, St. Buddha, *ora pro nobis* [pray for us]. Now, our heavenly Father never fails, with manna from heaven and the purple of lilies.

Being poor is a lovely dream. A sure road to the empyreal.

In a touching reminder, look to the image of a camel passing through the eye of a needle . . . and the rich man entering the gates of hell . . .

The church was doing a total reversal now and teaching that poverty was a scourge invented by the rich. The needle did an about-face and went up the camel's backside. . . . An impressive maneuver by the new knights of the Gospel. Nobel Peace Prize! This is not a prophecy or an epistle to the liking of an elitist Christianity. Its purpose is to condemn the rich, the apocalyptic multinational industries that brought the plague of hunger back to the planet. They forget the poor humble-at-heart rich, and the poor born with the spirit of barons.

We forget that every man came into the world with the abilities and instruments adequate to earning a living. If not like the lilies of the field and the birds in the sky, at least like bees and ants, like fishes, crustaceans in the mangroves, and batrachians in the lakes. We forget that nature is beautiful and rich in resources. Instead of throwing stones at the rich, planters of hunger, what is needed is to awaken in the poor the dormant abilities to gain their daily bread with the sweat of their brows. Even today, no bee has ever been seen begging by the side of the road. Nor homeless ants attempting to take over the anthills of others. Or Marxist locusts preaching redistribution of assets. The critics of the rich should teach the poor the power of sweat and the magic of work. The miracle of a seed, born because someone decided to plant it. There are no riches in the world, there is nothing in the world that can withstand the sweat spread over the land, in which "planting, everything grows . . ." The soil is told: take and eat, this is my blood, which will be spilled for a piece of bread.

There is subtle method in the art of begging. Which obeys a simple reasoning and deceptive deduction. Only men are capable of the deed. As well as cats and dogs, but only after learning it from their owners. The universal premise is that there is always someone who takes pleasure in giving alms. Giving for the sake of giving. Or because they enjoyed it and took a liking to the supplicant. What matters is the expression on the recipient's face. The rest is of no interest. Whether it is needed, or not. In fact, there is an outpouring of the soul of him who gives, both to one who has not or to him who has. The Book of Job is written unconsciously in the heart of man. Truly, without that psychic inscription, books would not exist. Other animals, which neither ask for nor receive alms, must struggle from first to last breath to keep from starving to death. With talon, prudence, and great stubbornness. Like the maria-farinha crab on the beaches of the Northeast.

Putting an end once and for all to the mystique that poverty leads to heaven isn't difficult. The Nordic countries barely recognize it. You don't play around with cold, snow, and ice. The birds of the sky depart for tropical climes. And the lilies of the field hide away to hibernate. Buddha flees. Impossible to sit cross-legged on the edge of the sidewalk.

It's time for things to go back. We must have the courage to declare that it is easier for a camel to pass through the eye of a needle than for the indolent poor to save themselves. Hear Christ condemning the Pharisees: "Why trouble ye the woman? for she hath wrought a good work upon me. For ye have the poor always with you; but me ye have not always." It is necessary to note that Christ makes no distinction between the poor by choice and style of life and the blameless unfortunates who fell into poverty. To which they were fettered. Without knowing how to escape it but persisting in the art of gaining their daily bread. Others, however, lack the slightest intention to persist. No amount of riches in the world would make them give up their calling. Society has the obligation to wake them up and demonstrate the necessity of comfort and the beauty of well-being. And to toss in the trash the myth of the birds and the lilies. Unlike the Preacher on the mount. After all, it's not like that. If it's true that not even Solomon ever dressed in such a fashion, and that they neither weave nor sew, the Messiah forgets that the progenitor of the lilies labored endless nights and long days to see his son clothed that way. The purple represents in fact a generous wage for a skillful court seamstress. Nor is it true that the Heavenly Father intercedes to feed the birds of the skies. In every part of the world, they have to rise early and work hard from morning till evening in search of food. From which one can conclude that the Messiah exaggerated a bit, naturally with the best of intentions, exposing himself to erroneous and dangerous interpretations. For He was not preaching to anyone: don't work! He was merely saying: Concern yourself with today; let tomorrow be, as do the birds in the sky and the lilies of the field.

Chapter Three

I came to learn that those hippies were not actually muscular and violent roughnecks, Hell's Angels, demons on two wheels who on their motorcycles swept along highways, frightening everyone, attacking, raping, robbing, with public order unable to do anything; not even the insolent beatniks, claiming to be poets and prophesying barbarous things, or simply the bums who were a living challenge to any kind of order, respect, cleanness and work, with their epic and thundering belches, spitting gum in people's faces, hawking phlegm on the sidewalk, grabbing incautious females and taking them to their boyfriends, or even reformist intellectuals or malcontents of every stripe and variety who began everywhere to spread the rules and anti-rules from the primer of the good life, their customs, right and left, their way and nobody's way. *"Vive la merde! Citoyen, il faut épater Madame, la Manière!"* ["Long live the shit! Citizen, we must flabbergast Madame, the Manner!"]

At Woodstock, they spat in the face of the times and traditions, all that civilization had established safe and dear, and society deemed sacred and holy. The order of the day was to confront the "squares," to bury alive all who opposed their outrages.

I verified immediately that this was a different people. By their habits, their manner, their refinement and politeness. Musicians, poets, playwrights, priests, monks, two nuns, two or three seminarians, and a Jew with curly braided hair. Like the Essenes in the days when Christ was only a crazy beatnik.

Beethoven is said to have conceived the *Sixth Symphony* beside the ocean. Shakespeare wrote *The Tempest* listening to the waves. There was, among them, a deep-seated notion that once the human voice is set free, it is nevermore lost. It was the voice of Christ from the Sermon on the Mount that the plainclothes priests, nuns, and seminarians persevered in espousing. Their miniature recorders at the ready, eyes closed in eternal concentration, fingers erect like antennas.

Someone once understood clearly and distinctly Cicero as he inveighed against a senatorial colleague: "*Quousque tandem abutere, Catalina, patientia nostra? Quandiu iste furor tuus nos illudet?*" ['How long will our patience last, Catalina? How long will this fury of yours mock us?'] The emotional eloquence with which it was declaimed, the tone of voice and the richness of modulation in the pronunciation of the diphthongs in *quousque* and *quandiu*, all of it captured and recorded verbatim for the eternal delight of those who cultivate the dead language. People have praised the acoustics of the Roman senate. And the playful asides that merged shrewdness and the sarcasm of *patres conscripti*, the lovely designation for senators, heroes with excellent souls, duly recruited to render services to the fatherland in the fields of science or battle.

How beautiful was the form of address of the Romans, by chance so well preserved in our time. A senate hearing might well devolve into a rerun of the Far West. "*Patres conscripti!* Your Excellency is a son of a bitch!" And another, "*Patres conscripti*, a senator's dishonor can only be washed away with blood. Bang! Bang! Bang!"

But the Law, which renders everyone equal, respects the dignity of our noble *Pater*, elected under the threat of tyranny, O simpleton ... have you never heard of a lady called Dona Hunger, queen in these parts?! Menace, its mere mention, assures the election of the new Pater, to whom the Law grants, in addition to other things, the bonus of immunity. Thus, the Law engages in masturbation and suicide, offering paradise to the very ones who deform, rape, and assassinate it. *Kyrie eleison!* Free us, Lord, from our senators!

Someone managed to catch Demosthenes with pebbles in his mouth. Taming the crashing of the waves in order to become the most famous orator of antiquity.

Unfortunately, there is no evidence of the voice of Christ. Or of the mob shouting "We want Barabbas!" The Jew had also abandoned his post, disillusioned and unhappy. He had spent an entire year without succeeding on hearing the voice of Jehovah dictating the commandments, and handing the Tablets of the Law to Moses. He would return later. He always returned. The faith of Abraham never dies in the Hebrew heart. The epic moment of Jewish history had to yield to his ever-vigilant ears. Fight, fight, Jacob, until the angel surrenders.

The priests also never became frustrated. How could they, who live to sow the faith? The nuns raised their arms and extended their delicate hands to the sky. The youngest of them looked like a gypsy. She wore light lipstick. In addition to earrings and necklaces under the imposing hat of a sister of charity. A great nun. Underneath, her perky breasts pushed against her habit, trying to gain the freedom to proclaim the magnificence of the Gospel. What infidel in the world could resist the epiphany of such breasts?

The seminarian leapt to the highest rock and stationed himself there, closest to the sky, legs spread and barefoot, in a capoeira position. His vivacity failed to attract the benevolence of the Almighty, involved in a serious discussion of the just up in Heaven. Not a single angel came forth to soothe his head, which was beginning to bleed, or at least to praise his balance. Those convictions customarily die like that, without drawing the slightest attention of the On High, habituated to the routine of fasting and self-flagellation. In other words, as if to say the Kingdom of Heaven does not bow to quibbles.

There, no one spoke to anyone. They did not see one another, nor communicate among themselves, as if the others didn't exist. Not even me, motionless and gazing in wonder at what I saw. Then a disturbance arose among them. It was the taking of Troy, no less, that the learned man in the wide-brimmed hat had captured in the moment. His companion, however, resolutely denied this; it was the destruction of Sodom and Gomorra, beyond any doubt. Another positioned himself between the pair, screaming, gesticulating, readying a blow as if to knock teeth out of both and insisting that all the hubbub could only come from the Tower of Babel, if not from the burning of Rome. The priest, who was fat and peaceful, sitting in his corner, was nodding his head and opining merely that it might also be the decapitation of innocent saints or the Egyptian mothers lamenting the death of their firstborn.

I continued on my way, rather distressed by the absurdity of the divergent opinions about such grievous moments for the human race, when, suddenly, I seemed to hear a low, grave voice dolorously repeating:

"Eli! . . . Eli! . . ." followed by indistinct words in the Syrian language that sounded like ancient Aramaic.

I thought to myself: "Maybe they were right. Even though

they understood nothing. Perhaps all of human history was lost in particles of sound drifting in a space that we don't know."

Chapter Four

I went no farther. At the moment, I did nothing at all, thinking myself the victim of collective suggestion. As I've said, I didn't know how I had come to end up in that spot. I don't believe I had attained what joggers call "runner's high." In which, after fifteen to twenty minutes the mind expands and elevates, and we feel above ourselves, our head seems to volatize, and our body starts to fly. The step becomes light, the legs barely touching the ground. We plunge into an atmosphere in which we no longer feel our body. The mind takes the body on ethereal wings and flies in powerful, indescribable bliss. Voices in the heights seem to call us by name, converse with us as if they knew us from the beyond. Everything an amalgam of ineffable sensation that would elude the most brilliant pen and the cleverest imagination.

I confess that, consciously. I never achieved that state of pure bliss. Even though I strove like a donkey aspiring to fly. And there were instants when I felt I was on the verge of transcending myself. In a nearly-nearly of elevating myself beyond. I would make a few small cathodic leaps, some equine thrusts, weird in nature but serious in intent, ridiculous in any case to whomever might see me. Dying for my mind to lift me into the air. Surprising me when I said softly:

"O mind, go! Seize me! At least for an instant!"

To no effect. Nothing, nothing. My pachyderm mind remained flaccid, slow, and without ardor. It ignored the impulse to fly. Because a voice spoke in my ears, without my being able to identify what it was, whether a noise from the waves, or the spheres, with its jumble of indistinct voices.

I knew that the Potter, when He made me, was dead tired, as he left me all twisted and out of place. And his breath was short. Instead of entering through the nostrils, it escaped through the forehead. Still a child, I was balder than my grandfather. Who, like me, had come out asymmetrical from head to feet. With one brown eye and one black. The left one could see at a distance, the right one, up close. One foot walked forward, the other, sideways. One side of my face came from my father, the other, from my mother. The brow, the best of the three, belonged to a masturbating uncle. Sincere. Resolute. Arrogant. Prisoner of his ecstasy. Praying and seeing wanton images before him. The heavens opening through the work of his hands. He had written philo-theological treatises about it. A posthumous work found inside a pillow. He considered orgasm something sublime and holy, not to be shared with anyone. He died a virgin, buried by virgins who futilely adored him. The next day, his grave was found covered with beautiful yellow butterflies fluttering their wings. Belonging to the new order of butterflies, sisters of masturbation. Some parts, exclusively mine, dwarves at retail, colossal at wholesale. In general, they all came from the most diverse and varied types of the family.

Now, my legs left donkey tracks in the sand. My lungs laboring like a steam locomotive. Lips on fire, nostrils smoking. The old blood-mover desperate and bellowing "Stop that shit!" Which really shocked me. My heart, always polite and respectful, had never been profane or spoken like that. I often remembered La Fontaine repeating *"Tu n'as pas d'ailes et veux voler, rampe!"* ["You've got no wings and you want to fly, crawl!"] Which, beyond a doubt, I deserved to hear. Whoever lacks wings and wants to fly ends up eating mud. I paused to meditate the vengeance of my enfeebled heart.

The fact is that I had never given credence to that story of soaring in the clouds. And, to tell the truth, no voice ever reached my ears to invite me to fly. But, so as not to conflict with the Epicureans, let's just say I nearly, nearly achieved that sublime state, feeling now and then some slight effects of that vaunted bliss, sufficient to make me forget myself and pass the return point. That must have been it, I'm certain it was.

Chapter Five

I noticed that the long and picturesque beach curved again and shrank, as if wishing to bar my passage. Enormous rocks began in the ocean and came toward the beach, in a procession of misshapen, crippled stones born in the depths of the sea, crashing into impulsive waves whipped into a frenzy by the wind, raising their voices, lifting their arms and shaking their skirts. They were like angry housewives fighting at an outdoor market, trying to prevail by roughhousing and by yelling the loudest. Waves and wind, rolling, rolling, in lascivious pelvic thrusts, or simply trotting in an elegant quadrille. Afterwards, the winds departed, and the waves flattened, abandoned and accepting. Murmuring softly whatever it was in their language. Until they too went away, leaving behind the rocks, once again the absolute masters of the landscape.

At that moment, a sly sun, the blond German of the spheres, appeared. In love with the color of wheat, even if it was the color of the rocks. A simple creature, however, for all his pomp and splendor. "Bored with his gilded vault, he lamented not having been born a simple firefly," in the poetry of a great shaper of words from these regions.

I did not resist either. I went into the sea with long strokes, eager to stretch out on the rocks. The largest and prettiest of all, purple, smooth, reclining. A masterpiece of a rock contrasted with its neighbors. Monstrous, hunched, Quasimodesque, ferine, like brown reefs, the haunted manse of Northeast crabs.

Apprehension assailed me at that instant. To make certain I was alone, I looked around. Nonsensical apprehension that sometimes comes over me, thinking someone is with me. I lay down. crossed my hands over my chest. Closing my eyes, I began to wander through all my weary senses. And, decisively, brushed aside the grotesque philosophy of transcendent corridors.

Chapter Six

At first, I was unable to differentiate the sound coming from the waves on the rocks from the murmur of the winds. I was uncertain whether they were resuming the eternal litany or whether it was a remnant of fractured voices in the vault of Heaven. But gradually they became distinct. Ever so slowly, I changed positions to the other side of the rock. The sight was astonishing. I was incredulous, numb, parched and cross-eyed. For there, I saw a shark huge beyond description, a colossal gray shark, body half out of the water, above the fins, speaking, gesturing in a most entertaining chat—with a stupid mud worm. An insignificant thing. Nevertheless, as lovely as could be. Lying down, relaxed and self-assured, exposed to the kisses of the blond German of the spheres, addicted to the dark-complected.

Byron once gave thanks to the heavens over the lack of a worthy metaphor for the foot and ankle of a señorita from Cádiz. And I, whom should I thank for not having a single image capable of describing the most beautiful earthworm in the world, whose skin and voluptuous movement never had their painters, and challenged sculptors, mocked poets? Where were the Gauguins of my land? The Di Cavalcantis? The Cícero Diases? Where were the painters of genius when one is needed? And poets? Where are the likes of César, of Accioli, of Francisco Bandeira? Where are Déborah and Lenilde, the grand dames of the poetry of Recife? What are you doing, Francisco Brennand, with your fiery genius, your epic poem in clay? I ceased my untimely apostrophes in order to concentrate on the most prosaic dialogue I have ever witnessed.

"Are you married, little one?" asked the shark in an impetuous and rich voice.

"Me? . . . Oh no! . . . At least not yet . . ."

My eyes ceased to blink, my ears to buzz, in my head a sense of the absurd ran roughshod over good sense. The son of Dona Philomena was affecting my mind, without a trace of doubt. What vision, what voices clouded my spirit? I rubbed my eyes, wondering what kind of jest it was, whether I was being taken for a fool or not. They, irritated, protested in unison: "We never lie!"

Arrogance of my eyes. Certain tenants, whom I esteem and who live on the top floor of the building, spend the day with their binoculars pointed at the world, sniffing out and annotating everything with the precision of accountants, but yes or no, there was a small snake.

I remembered that as a young child, playing alone on the beach sand, my mother, serious and concerned, cautioned me: " . . . Be wary, my son, of the mermaids' song!" "What are mermaids, mother?!" "Sirens of the sea, my son. From the waist up, they have the body of a beautiful woman, long hair floating in the water; from the waist down, the tail of an enormous fish covered with scales. Anyone who doesn't run away from their song gets dragged to their castle at the bottom of the ocean. . . ."

The fascination awakened in me had the opposite effect, and since then I would give anything to see a mermaid. How I would like one of them to take me to her golden castle in the depths of the sea! . . . Later I learned that, instead of love, they offered immortality. (This to me, who was so afraid of dying!) As Calypso had proposed to Ulysses, and he rejected, crazy Greek that he was. He could have benefited from a complete brain transplant.

Now was I, a grown man, bearded and all, actually hearing that? Truthfully, it was an earthworm such as you see only once in a lifetime. A chromatic, melodious voice, golden cords vibrating. A bit unsure of herself. Moving slowly, petrified. An innocent young thing in her first courtship. A most curious bait. I got comfortable so as not to miss a word of the transcendent dialogue. I remained infinitely unmoving, planning to stay there only to sunbathe, nothing more, nothing less. Then I heard the shark's provocative line:

"How can it be, little one? How can the males here leave you all alone? With that doll's body, that poppy skin! It's enough to drive people mad, little one! It can't be! It can't be, I don't believe it!"

"Little one?" Where did that come from? The expression and the treatment, the way he talked? His tongue, completely extended, began hitting the roof of his mouth in an uncontrolled fever of desire. Shameless as could be, the shark. It was quickly apparent that he was one of those who had no respect for females. Even mixing daily tasks with the customary idleness, and wherever he went and whomever he encountered, there he played the show-off and the buffoon. The worm, on the other hand, blushed. The blood gushing through her veins, suspended. Not knowing how to extract herself from that situation. Finally, with difficulty, she smiled, and her tongue loosened for good:

"Me? Huh! . . . Poor me, who doesn't know what it's like to be away from home. If I step outside, my brothers jump all over me. I'm an 'airhead,' they say, who never thinks and doesn't have any sense. They never forgive me for anything in life, from the day I escaped from home and entered a beauty contest. I paraded on the runway. And I was crowned queen. The applause that followed hasn't left my mind. It almost caused me to faint. The ovations. The lights shining on me. The whistles and cheers. I was hugged, kissed, tossed in the air. Afterwards we paraded in the streets and a group of foreign women applauded me the whole time and formed a block, dancing the samba and singing as if it were Carnival in their land. The people in a delirium trying to keep up with the music and the delirious steps:

> We, we, we,
> We the earthworms
> Here on Earth, we call the shots
> And when things get tough
> It's worms they like the best.
>
> No need to be ashamed
> Feel free to show shame
> Your booty
> 'Cause for Mister
> Life just changed
> For us, for us . . .
>
> All Recife wants to embrace us
> The little earthworms
> And when we get going
> It's a clinch they really go for.

"Raising their chest and spreading their arms in the feverish movement of the samba, they broke into another melody:

Worms, we're Brazilians
We live under just one flag
Let's sing and live our glory
Earthworms! Earthworms! Earthworms!

"The people applauded, asked for an encore, and memorized without understanding what they were singing.

"I miss the songs and my Brazilian colleagues. Happy, free, with their souls in their hands. They opened a world for me I didn't know. I received countless proposals . . . poor people, rich people, a general, a diplomat, even a senator, old, paunchy, lame in one leg, nice as the devil and cheeky like you never saw.

"In the midst of all that, flowers, hugs, kisses, I laughed and cried from happiness. Ah, I'll never forget that night. When I close my eyes, it all comes back to me in memory, as if I were there at that instant, the Brazilian women singing and dancing in the streets." For a few instants, the earthworm really did close her eyes, allowing herself to be swept away by the dream of her life. She had the soul of a butterfly and wanted to be a ballerina. She pictured herself on stage, twirling, twirling, enraptured, leaving only a shadow in a transformation of matter overcoming gravity and rising into the sky.

"At the break of day," she continued, after a long sigh, "when I set foot in the house, my brothers were waiting at the door. They skinned me alive. The boy who brought me suffered a beating that nearly killed him. Poor thing, tall and thin, he fought like a beast against the three of them. Parrying and returning the blows. He was bleeding when he left. I'll never forget Diolito, his courage and bravery. We met twice more, hiding in the dark. Fearful of being discovered. On the third time, my youngest brother, the worst of them all, caught us. They beat me to a pulp. That same night, they tried to dump me in a convent. After a lot of harassment, 'Hit her, hit her, she's got no sense,' my mother agreed. They were going to shut me away in a few days. In the strictest place there was. I couldn't even choose which order.

"I cried, entire nights, soaking the pillow. My fate. My destiny. I wanted to die. Later, very gradually, a light appeared in the depth of my reason. I began to pretend, pretending I was convinced, looking at the convent as something holy and beautiful, appropriate to my nature. I went further. I prepared my face, both inside and out. I expanded my expression, adopted a mystic gaze. Smiling with my eyes, pressing my lips. I made them believe there had been born in me a vocation to be a nun. That the life of a virgin dedicated to prayer and higher things now attracted me. At night, I would hear that voice. Even dreaming, I would hear, 'Come! Come!!' Calling me to the convent to change my life. It would be my destiny. Only then would I be happy.

"They were convinced. They smiled at me for the first time in my life. They called me 'Dona Freira,' 'Sor Monice,' 'my sister the nun,' or 'little sister of the heart!' Even my mother fell in line. They embraced me. Brought sweets and flowers. Women friends and neighbors did the same. They made me a gift of a Carmelite habit and persuaded me to wear it. For a whole month. For an entire month I lived the Carmelo life, right there at home. With fasting, meditation and everything.

"I did all the preparation, spoke with nuns who praised my vocation and were anxiously awaiting me. I began stripping away neighbors, friends, and acquaintances. I wept with them as we hugged. Still, it was never my intention to end up inside there. Before crossing the threshold, I planned to run away. I would rendezvous with Diolito. Hide in a corner, live with him in any part of the world. I wrote him two messages detailing everything, day, time, meeting place. He never answered. I don't know if he received them. I had never seen him again. Nor could I imagine what had become of him. Whether he died or is still alive, if he sent a note to me, my brothers would have destroyed it and gone after him. My brothers are wild animals, savages. As if I were their daughter. Worse than my father, who deserted my mother when I was little. If not for my mother, I would have died at their hands.

"A happy night, an unhappy night, the beauty contest! I was a prisoner all that time. The worst punishment in life is a brother's jealousy. My father was a doctor who fought a lot with my mother but he never beat me, never. My mother too, so loving, except when I give her a reason."

The shark didn't know what to say. He made a vague movement with his head, whether to show solidarity and compassion, or merely from upset and surprise. In fact, completely moved and emotional. Meanwhile, she continued in the same tone.

"The great day had arrived. I got up early. That premonition always with me. I said goodbye, weeping, hugged my mother and, sobbing, begged them not to follow me. I didn't want to be seen crying in the street. Reluctantly, they granted me my last request.

"I took the seaside path. But woe is me! As soon as I set foot on the beach, a wave caught me and I ended up here. I was almost smashed on the rocks. Now, with no idea of what my life will be, how I can get back when night comes and the sea rises. They're surely going to think I ran away. And if they find Diolito, poor thing, if he's still alive, he'll be beaten to death. It's as if I can see him, in a fight to the death, brave as a bull, confronting my brothers."

"Look, my little one, don't fret! Now you're with me, and in these parts I'm the king. See my size, my muscles? No one can stand up to me!" (He swelled his chest, flexed his fins, exhibiting himself like a circus strong man, did a few somersaults, and came to a stop showing his teeth.) "When I raise my tail," he continued, "even the waves flee in terror. Have no fear, little one, no one here would take you away from me. As for your people back home, well . . . I'll take you back and have a word or two with those brothers of yours . . . Don't think about it for now . . . How about a short outing on the beach? Just jump onto my shoulder and, in an instant, we'll be at one of the most picturesque spots on the coast. What do you say?"

And he was about to run his hand over her body. She recoiled. And he rebuked himself, thinking he had moved too fast. In amorous conquests, the most important thing was not to go too fast. He always forgot that. He opened his mouth and there went that hand, ruining everything. He noticed she was still cowering, her expression still somewhat unhappy, absent, saying something to herself in a small voice, and for a long time mute, which tortured him cruelly, seeing her motionless, lost inside herself.

Her mind began to wander through a world of apprehensions, a lost past, so distant that it wasn't hers, all that her mother had told her as a young girl, coming back in a whirlwind of memories both happy and distressing.

Chapter Seven

The voice came from the chest, suddenly, speaking now with her eyes fixed on him. Taking this is a sign, he drew nearer, on the pretext of hearing better.

She was a noble, her blue blood came from the origins of the world. The first animal to appear on the planet. The chrysalis in which the plants transformed. She descended directly from the first woman, to whom the Great Kyrios said: "Let there be the earthworm!" Like a princess of the animals of the earth. Part of a superior class from which came the chameleons, the lizards, even the serpents, arrogant cousins, envious, lying, full of malice and venom in their mouths. Treacherous like none other, because of them misfortune entered the world. Misfortune entered the world. Be wary.

It behooves us to say, however, that the brains of it all was Eve, with her genius for inventing and fantasizing things. Telling stories. Yes, her unforgettable stories. Engrossing. Which left indelible marks on people's souls.

Eve told stories. At the end of the day, to amuse us, all the people, animals, mosquitos sat down to listen. Even the trees fell silent, suppressing the slightest sigh. In her lovely voice, her flowery language, her fingers traced in the air what her words contained. The children and the animals shouting, demanding more, and the grown-ups applauding and voicing encouragement:

"Bravo, Eve! Bravo! Bravo! Tell us another, Aunt Eve, tell it!"

And the giraffe, nibbling on something or other, raising his chin, concluded nasally, "Tell us! Tell us, woman!" And the ass, inventor of the encore, when he sounded his Heehaw! Heehaw! Heehaw! All with frightful impertinence.

Because there was no one who could stand the tiresome discourse of the crickets and the cicadas, alternating without a pause with the bands of toads hidden in the thicket, in a futile attempt to replace the songbirds and entertain at day's end. The latter belonged to the musicians' union, which forbade them to sing at night. The owl was also a card-carrying member, but everyone detested his voice and style, and from one rejection to the next, the unfortunate bird had to accept the night shift, which no one wanted, but even so he could only sing when everyone else was already asleep. Without the least loss to anyone, for not a single animal complained, as his voice was a mournful omen, resembling a soul in torment, haunted by ghosts and nightmares. Someone woke up in fright and threw stones at him. He fled. "Go sing like that in some bawdyhouse, you foreboding good-for-nothing," cried irate voices. The poor animal avoided the stoning, until one rock hit him in the face and broke his beak. The right-minded folk objected, arguing it wasn't something you do to an animal that hurts no one. They saw a sign in the owl's sinister gaze, called him the sybil of the night, bearer of messages of future misfortunes. A living symbol of wisdom. Which is why, filled with that same spirit, spokesmen of ill-omened learning and prophecies, modern philosophers proudly display his effigy on their fingers.

No one could tell stories like Eve with her unique way of imagining and coloring things. Four, five, six stories a night weren't enough to meet the demand. Sometimes they would talk all night and continue the next day. She would tire, her throat dry. The people would rush to bring her coconut water, juice of the mangaba, or passionfruit. The children and the smaller animals, forever a nuisance, asking for another, one more. For it was always the children who wanted to hear stories ceaselessly. Her repertoire exhausted, Eve invented the idea of "representing" the episodes she related, preferring animals and children to grown-ups. Which resulted in severe criticism and no small amount of enmity. She tried to involve a greater number of people and animals. Thus, they were satisfied with a single presentation per night. This is how theater came about as a form of entertainment. First in the outdoors and, when it rained, in caves. Animals with talent became important figures, or "stars," hailed and sought-after by people when they set foot outside. In this way, the parrot and the monkey achieved greatness. Later, others—more slow-witted and lazier but determined to master the art—were recognized at last and applauded. Even a mixed-breed owl had his pleasant role. With his flexible personal magnetism, he was a triumph on stage. His eyes and his song rang in the dark nights in which everything combined to transport the audience to a world of revelations. He represented the dawn of time and the apocalypse. His voice moaned in the din of death, a chorus of two voices declaimed the tragedy, while a third, in *bouche fermée*, expressed the emotion and suspense that invaded everything. With his talent for summoning dreams, invoking things that were and were not, and would come to be. Or, as such, would never come but became visible and palpable in the grave melody of his sinister song. And, through this, they would eventually see in him the incarnation of austere wisdom.

Among the stars, the most talented, the prima donna of

the stage was naturally the earthworm, envied by the serpent, applauded by the Great Kyrios, and kissed on the cheek by Adoné in the time she courted Jupiter, the Lord Kyrios of Olympus. Hearing talk of the theater starring an earthworm, he attended with Adoné, insistently desirous of taking her to Greece. Jupiter, who at the time was called Zeus, would copy everything in order to teach it to the Greeks, his chosen people on Earth to excel in all arts and sciences.

That, however, would be much later... (The shark here made an aside to say that his cousin, the dolphin, was outstanding in athletics and all types of magic. In addition to his humanitarian work of saving drowning people, to the displeasure of the majority, who saw in it a leftist tendency. The dolphins were sincere in what they did and were considered by all as the mystics of the seas, so the sharks thought it best to leave them in peace. However, the champions in devouring legs and arms were the whales ... Their legitimate cousin, the myth of the seas...)

The earthworm showed signs of displeasure so she wouldn't be interrupted. All of that was true, but it wasn't the time to bring it up. "Please, Mr. Shark!"

"Ah! Excuse me, my little one, I have yet to introduce myself ... My name is Clytorino, but you can call me Clyto. Perhaps from a defect of the tongue that comes from my grandparents." (He laughed awkwardly, pressing his lips together and hiding his tongue inside.) The earthworm turned red, the color of a burning coal, saying:

"Ah! Pleased to meet you, Clyto! My name is Monice..."

"Charmed, Monice!... Forgive the interruption..."

"Not at all, imagine! It seems like a dream, at a time like this, to fall into the hands of someone who takes an interest in me..."

Smiling, he bowed elegantly, with highly refined taste. Beginning to show himself to be a bundle of contradictions, our elasmobranch with his torpedo body and his hippopotamus mouth, now gentlemanly and seductive, now arrogant, swaggering, and bloodthirsty. A macho down to the marrow of his bones. Now still witty, very polite, incredibly cultured and well read. As if he had frequented the world's famous universities. But the first impression persisted: a cunning dandy after an easy conquest.

Chapter Eight

"Now," Eve said, "let's go back a couple of millennia and we're going to relate some unpublished episodes in the history of the world. Make yourselves comfortable where you are, as we're ready to take off," she said humorously, modifying her tone for effect and to create suspense. "Those with limited intelligence should leave now, or not bother me with foolish ideas, nausea and headaches." There was a certain uneasiness, a stirring of assent, nervous whispers, but curious, amazed, and anxious to know, no one left...

"All was darkness," Eve continued, closing her eyes and seeking the voice lost in her breast, "darkness, only darkness in endless space, when the first light appeared. Slowly at first. Randomly. That trace of light. A trace, because it had no body, just a trace, no expression to describe that piece of things. Except it wasn't light yet, and no one knew what it was. It was just the 'Thing.' The 'white thing,' indescribable. No one had ever seen anything like it. All prideful, full of itself. It asked Darkness:

"'Who are you? What are you doing here? And what blackness is that all over your body?'

"Darkness replied to her face: 'No concern of yours!' And left hurriedly to tell others that a weird stranger had just appeared, all knowledgeable and complicated. Intrusive as could be, presumptuous, wearing a color never seen before. Clutching onto everything. Unlike them. Conceited. An outlandish skin and finding theirs strange.

"'That's the last thing we needed! . . . Not good at all!' everyone shouted. 'Who is that idiot? Where did it come from?'

"No one knew. 'In any case . . . you must be careful,' said the eldest one. 'People like that, butting into the lives of others, trying to find out about yours, could be the end of everything. Goodbye to privacy, goodbye to peace, goodbye to a calm life!'

"From then on, whenever they encountered it, they would look at it sideways, hiding in the corners. Every time they saw the 'Thing' approaching, they fled, without it knowing where they had gone. The 'Thing' followed them, trying to be friends. Darkness did not consent, not believing in that futile friendship, not allowing itself to be overtaken. It shrugged, clicked its tongue disdainfully, and vanished! It habitually ridiculed any expressive impertinence. Deep down, it was apprehensive. There was no way it could allow itself to be taken by the strange viscous 'Thing.' Not even by drawing close and discovering who it was. That viscosity, that transparent skin irritated Darkness. And, out of disdain, it was given the name 'Light,' the most repellent designation to be found in its vocabulary. Because it truly shone, spread itself, transcended, in a garish, irritating way. Making everything clear. Stripping Darkness nude. The nudity of Darkness was the most sacred thing that existed, where it kept the maximum of confidentiality. For Light to violate it was a confrontation, a damnable act of gall.

"Darkness was wily by nature, self-aware and, because it existed before anything else, harbored an incredibly unshakable sense of superiority in relation to the rest. The master of everything, including of Light. Who detested the role of subaltern. And the more Light advanced, the further Darkness withdrew. It looked inside itself and increased the awareness of its infinite secret. It took pride in its dark skin. In contrast to Light, within itself it saw the shadow of immortality. Compared to it, Light was an ephemeral phenomenon, useless and devoid of the density Darkness possessed. A mere accident of being. Not a tranquil being in itself. To be Darkness, on the other hand, was to be a complete Being, the Being par excellence. A Being truly a Being. To be Light was merely a happening in the dark, an accidental and fortuitous event. With no permanent duration. Because in fact it never existed and only now arrived there in front of Darkness, which in the sphere of such thought felt like a Kyrios in person, alive, eternal, infallible, with no rival in excellence or even possible. Its dominion extended throughout endless space. Where nothing that was not darkness existed. Nor could exist. If Light wanted to approach, first it must turn itself off and become equal to Darkness. Or else explode from envy. Jealousy. Internal dissatisfaction.

"Thus, Light angrily came to call Darkness savage, ignorant, brutish. In return, Darkness termed it 'the white Thing,' disgusting, repellent, foolish, and intrusive. War to the death was declared. So it was in the beginning. Like Romulus and Remus when they founded Rome.

"Indignant, Light racked its brain to discover the mystery of its enemy. It took years, centuries and countless unending millennia.

"Once, rubbing together two pieces of darkness that were floating past, Light saw a spark. It rubbed harder and harder, and suddenly the spark became a flame. And the flame was fire, and the fire was like an image of itself. The fire was Light. It was a tremendous revelation. A marvel. As if Light had reproduced itself. Had Light been born of Darkness and were they sisters?!

Or, actually, mother and daughter? Light was going to surprise Darkness when it was resting and relate what happened, tell it they possessed the same nature. Which, though sincere, was an enormous presumption. Certain that, by so doing, it would put an end to the ill will. All it accomplished, however, was to make Darkness more indignant than ever and, seeing itself attacked, flee even further. And there was no way to coax it to come closer so it could be examined. Ensconced in its infinite vault like a black Kyrios, diaphanous and solemn, unknown to itself and everything. Nevertheless, invincible. Never accepting sharing its realm with anyone, feeling more than ever its indomitable power. And saying: 'We, the Darkness, and beside us, no one!' And repeated: 'Our nature and our essence are one and indivisible! Beyond us, only absolute chaos!' It didn't even try to understand who Light was, desiring simply to disdain the existence of the irritating, contagious and repulsive 'white Thing.'

"Light fell into a tremendous state of indignation, furiously racking its brain over the obstinate behavior of Darkness. Not, however, giving up, and seeking at all costs to solve the mystery that so provoked and anguished it, Light resolved to go to work again, succeeding through great effort in increasing the fire that, in addition to brightening everything, devoured whatever was before it. 'Go forth, besiege the Darkness,' she said, like a king sending his son against the enemy. Then, after sweeping the world, fire returned extinct and disillusioned, buffeted by the infinite, enslaving and monstrous Darkness, which celebrated its victory in the shadows. Darkness—invincible, immortal, sarcastic and more disdainful than ever, destroying any that approached and mocking those who would touch it.

"Then Light invented the oceans in order to surprise Darkness as it slept. And the failure was greater still. The waters became lost amid the Darkness, without know where they were or where they were going. They were pummeled, displaced from their lofty heights, screaming and forced to cast themselves over waterfalls, unsure of escaping alive, destined to form lakes, rivers, oceans.

"Light, after each defeat, became stronger, more imaginative, bolder, and more decisive.

"It didn't grow discouraged, and from the waters formed vapors, and from the vapors monstruous clouds that piled up in space and progressed like an army in battle.

"'After the enemy! After them!' ordered Light . . . rather successfully at first. For the clouds not only went after Darkness but also emitted stunning lightning bolts, stupendous blasts of steam that collided in thunderclaps and momentarily lit up everything, shook heaven and earth, opening a clearing in the center of Darkness like a nuclear blast, unmasking the invisible. Darkness had never trembled so much. For some instants, defeated and destroyed, its tactic was to flee and guffaw in response, 'Beside us, no one!' as if nothing had happened."

Strangely, Eve began to incorporate prophetic visions in these narratives, speaking of the future and the past and seeing everything as if in an album of images and paintings. The best of her fables, without a doubt, because visions of the future, or of the unknown past, always hold more fascination than anything in the present. The Great Kyrios, seated there, marveled at the fertileness of her imagination, her lucid and coherent visions, voicing them as they came to mind and seeing that what He had created was good, after all. Curious to know how far Eve's visions extended (Here the shark rudely interrupted to declare the woman, apparently more imaginative and creative than the man, because it was she and not Adam who knew these things, and it was therefore pure extortion on the part of the Great Kyrios to please his wife, Agapé. "From what we see, that was his intention, wasn't it, Monice?") He asked, but she didn't answer, as if she hadn't heard, and simply continued.

"Thus, millions of years went by, with the saga continuing always. Light, however, having never capitulated, as if its nature was to cast away Darkness, both created and uncreated, of whatever type, in any location, and had no other reason for existing, began to speculate what Darkness was like on the inside. What it was made of. What enigmatic nature it possessed. Its origin. Its reason for being. Its destiny. And concluded that Darkness must truly be eternal. Divine in both matter and its nature. And, as such, where it was and how it was had no beginning and would never end. Its palace, behind an impenetrable veil, was a conjuration that transcended the most lucid rationality, the most fertile fantasy. Here, it should be noted, many in the audience were beginning to experience delirium, suffering from headaches. Expressions of nausea and boredom.

"The German philosopher Novalis asked Night if it also possessed a human heart. I asked Darkness, or whoever could answer, if it was the Great Kyrios who created Darkness, or whether it was Darkness that created the Great Kyrios. Behold a transcendental mystery that challenges imagination itself," said Monice, in the grip of her own evocations.

Chapter Nine

Light, after having achieved such understanding, felt a shiver within. It felt anointed. And so happy that it split into two parts. And those two, into two more, and each of the two, into others. The nine Lights quickly fell to disagreeing among themselves, and with the first who had given them life. Some contended that Darkness was the Great Kyrios, who had created itself from nothingness. And from nothingness had created the world and everything else. Who continued, nonetheless, to dwell in the sky of Darkness, an enchanted palace, unimaginable to reason and the senses. That the Great Kyrios, King of Darkness, weary of its infinitude, created Light. He was enthralled and fell in love with it. And, from this happy collusion, created man in its image and the image of Light, giving him a little of everything, for himself and his consort. A bit of darkness, a bit of light. A bit of hatred, a bit of love. A bit of vengeance, a bit of forgiveness. A bit of fondness, a bit of cruelty. A bit of idleness, a bit of labor. A little bit of everything good, but not too much, so he would not become haughty, full of himself, and get the idea he was a kyrios equal to the Great Kyrios and rise up against Him.

But the new Lights always disagreed with the old. And they invented other stories based on the first. Darkness was a kyrios, yes, but without any trace of good. A black demon. A squalid monster. A ferocious seven-headed dog vomiting fire through seven mouths and seven noses. Seven rows of teeth in seven hungry mouths. Seven tumescent penises employed indiscriminately in seven vulvas in heat. Entities that inhabited the seven hells of the seven cursed whirlwinds. A place they created to torment themselves, according to some. To a demon, self-torment is like scratching oneself, a formidable pastime. Compared to which, any pleasure is torment. Still, they love pleasure. Because they adore tormenting themselves. By nature, by destiny, and by temperament. Condemned to suffer, enjoying and instigating enjoyment in every part of the world. To them, enjoyment is equal to suffering. So, they deliver every type of pleasure to their people.

This theory doesn't have many followers, but it has existed since the world began.

According to others, hell is a prison of fire and ice at the same time, fed by the deadly sins, especially pride, vanity, envy and greed, flaming wooden logs. The place to which the King of Darkness drags his enemies. And the more people who arrive, the greater grow the fire and ice.

Chapter Ten

The new Lights, thinking themselves the brightest of all, hated the past and invented still more novelties, mixing this and that, as they saw fit. In any case, they downplayed the differences and accentuated the similarities between the Great Kyrios and the enemies claiming the title of kyrios. Each with its angels, its armed and ferocious shield-bearers, fanatical followers of every type, size, and degree of cunning, for good and for evil, according to their propensity and their nature. Who spread throughout the world kidnaping adepts. Without realizing it, people found themselves in the middle of one group or another. But in the end the mixture was so great that the whole world is a conglomeration of angels beside devils, man being a bit of one thing and a bit of another. A little darkness, a little light, a little gold, a little mud. "Who does not the good he wishes, but the evil he abominates," in the words of a prophet who was blinded by a bolt of lightning but who, by rubbing mud in his eyes, regained his sight . . .

That man was Saul, the Moses of Christianity, the ingenious modality of the Judaism of Moses.

Here everyone interrupted, shouting:

"How can mud in the eyes improve vision?"

Eve replied that was how things would be in the future. There was magic called a miracle in which the laws of nature were suspended. Do not interrupt so she won't lose her way in the story. Nevertheless, a clamor was heard in the audience. Several people were spitting on the ground and rubbing mud in their eyes to clear up their sight. With disastrous results. They ran off, tripping as they went and booing, heading to a fountain to wash. At last, the shark, unable to contain himself, interrupted.

"Wait, Monice," he said, "there's a major error here. Saul never made mud with his own spittle to put into his eyes. It was Christ who did that to restore the sight of a man who was born blind. To prove he was sent by the Great Kyrios and to demonstrate his technical dominion over the elements."

"Look," she said, "know something once and for all, that an earthworm's memory is photographic and infallible. Not only for what she sees and hears, but what she smells, tastes and feels, or what just passes through her head. Our memory is ingrained, and limitless in space and time. Later you'll see why. I'm only repeating what was told by Eve and transmitted by our grandparents. It may be that in her prophetic vision she saw in Saul another Christ, even if he was different from the first. Because in reality there have been and still are many Christs in the world. We worms have ours too, just like the serpents and other animals have theirs. Each with his prophecies, his doctrines, his good and bad news. We have become accustomed to living surrounded by Christs. So much so that a world without Christs would be as empty as one without Moses, without Mohamed, without Buddha, without Confucius. Without the Kyrios of Olympus. A world blind and drab. But those two, Christ and Saul, besides being Jews, were the same size, with the type of heavy black beard of the transcendent mystics. Let's not criticize Eve for lacking the infallible memory of earthworms.

"Saul, however, was shrewd and didn't deserve the comparison. He emerged from blindness in order to heal the vision of those who saw well. According to him, Cephas and the others were introducing errors into the system to which they had been called. Cephas, the first Apostle and pope, who was called Peter, the cornerstone of the Church, was failing in his office as keeper of the keys. Of opening and closing the gates of the Kingdom, using the right key in the right keyhole of the lock. Perhaps because infallibility had yet to be invented. Which would come only after the discoveries of the Renaissance. Saul had no way of knowing about that. Despite the power of the keys given to Peter, that phrase 'all that you join together' perhaps meant something different. In his last moments of life, there was confusion and misunderstanding between Christ and the Father. He hesitated, lost spirit, asking and pleading that '. . . the chalice of the passion of redemption pass without his drinking of it . . .' He wept and even sweated blood. The reason for which the Father had become indignant. Thinking the Son had shown cowardice, he turned his face from him. On the cross, he cried out again, lamenting the abandonment . . . *'Eli! Eli! Lama sabachthani . . .'* ['My god! My god! Why hast Thou abandoned me . . .'] Furious, the Father cursed Him and swore never again to see Him. It was as if from the throne he exclaimed:

> 'You wept in the presence of the cross?
> Contemplating the crown, you wept?
> The Coward does not descend from the Strong.
> You wept, you are not my Son!
>
> Go Cursed and Alone in the world,
> For you came to such baseness
> That in the presence of death you wept,
> You, Coward, are no Son of mine!'"

In truth, during all the drama of the Passion, he had not appeared even once, nor said a word during the judgment and the death on the hill between two criminals. Nothing to comfort, nothing to reprehend, nothing. Just as if he didn't want to know about Him. That silence must have been his greatest torment. What father would close his eyes and leave his son alone in the hands of executioners, dying on a cross? The Old Father must have been truly ashamed, choosing to know nothing further about that Son.

To Saul, Cephas hadn't learned to use the keys and was unqualified for the job. Christ, as a consequence, regretted having selected him, finding him incompetent, and in order not to ruin the system, had given the keys to him. Saul had never known Christ while alive, *Kyrie eleison!* and if he had, would have had him stoned for blasphemy, just as had happened with Stephen. A crime he never confessed publicly, nor what had become of his clothing, holy relics, highly sought-after at that time, and today more precious than gold in the antiques market, one of the greatest treasures of the world and of Christianity. Similarly, Moses, who also never confessed the killing of the Egyptian, or David that of Urias (which makes us ponder, why that passion on the part of the Great Kyrios for choosing assassins as his prophets and leaders?). Beginning from then, Saul started to maneuver the Church toward his will. Disrespectfully, accusing Cephas of insincerity, both to his face and in public, something none of the true apostles, given the reverence they held for him, did or would do. A shortcoming he himself had committed, boasting orally and in writing. By subjecting that first living pope, sacred by the hands of Christ himself, to his visions and manias. This makes us wonder what a "Petrine" church would have been, in the style of the fishermen of Galilee, as intended by the founder, and not "Sauline," formulated by an adventurer impostor who forced his way into the Club of the Twelve Apostles. (He had for some unknown reason changed the name Christ himself had given him, Saul! Saul! . . . If he disdained the name given him by Christ himself, what respect would he have for Peter's?)

Saul, to enter the Club of Twelve, invented a fraudulent and implausible story. First, he seemed not to remember that the club wasn't twelve but thirteen. Judas had been the thirteenth, and the devil had taken him. For sure, he was unfamiliar with or attached little importance to the ancient legend that attributed the number thirteen to the demon.

The devil was an engineer famous for the construction of bridges. Because business was terrible in Hell, he decided to hold a promotion. He would build a bridge for whoever asked. Provided that the thirteenth person to cross the bridge was his. Once construction was complete and the celebrations over, he would place himself inconspicuously in a corner, counting and awaiting the thirteenth, who would be his payment. At first sight an awful bargain. At least in Germany, which breathed new life into the legend from bygone times. Later, he would gain some reimbursement when contracts were signed in Venice and Recife. No one understood how such an astute individual could have made so terrible a deal. The boarding houses and motels of Hell must be empty, waiting for lodgers and tourists. But there's an old saying: "Don't laugh at the devil and his motives, for he'll end up laughing at you." That dumb business about the bridges was in the end such a triumph as to leave Trump and Bill Gates looking like idiots. And the whole of Wall Street spinning chaotically. Because he carried off not only the first thirteenth person who came across the bridge but also every later thirteenth. From one side of the bridge to the other. From the river below to the sky above. From ships and submarines to airplanes and future satellites.

To the most highly credentialed biographer of the Demon, from Harvard, Cambridge, and the Sorbonne, and the wise men of the Gregoriana, the Zapelena, the Fuchs, the Healy, ensconced in the heart of the Vatican, the greatest puzzle today was a contract that he signed with George Washington. By which he would carry off the first virgin who crossed and all like her who might come later. Apparently the "great fox" knew his people better than the Prince of Darkness and taught him a lesson as good as what he had taught the redcoats. This was said to be the worst contract in the life of Old Scratch. One that from time to time makes him let out howls that shake the earth. They say the devil became so resentful that he tore up the papers in the face of the Yankee general and swore to sabotage the bridge someday. Something that to this day strikes fear in the heart of New Yorkers. Terrified by the disappearance of virgins and the demon's threats, they tried to import some, but the scarcity was the same everywhere. Thus, say the biographies, no one knows how much longer the suspense will continue, and who will have the last laugh, the astute demon or the American fox.

The fact is that Saul, without the least gift of prophecy, neither knew about nor foresaw any of this. In his mind, and that of others, he urged filling the vacancy left by Judas with a man worthy of Christ, and as soon as possible. Peter had already described the qualifications for the position. Naturally, the competition was great. Among the aspirants: Mark, his favorite; Luke, the preference of the others; Stephen, whose popularity was growing in the polls; Barnaby, who introduced Saul to the club and sponsored his candidacy; Lazarus, the preference of the rabble and women, the disciples from Emmaus, and even Gamaliel, the wise and prudent Jew, doctor of laws, would be a suitable candidate. They even discussed Mary of Bethania, who was the Grace Kelly of her day, after the Mother of Jesus adamantly opposed the launching of her own name. Which clearly proves that until then there was no need for a feminist movement.

Saul, a multifaceted genius, prevailed over everyone and gallantly won the place of Stephen, in all respects the strongest and most preferred candidate, who removed himself from competition by the simple process of being stoned to death. Rare but effective, following the law of Moses. After that, who would confront a man like him, bloody, ill-tempered, unpredictable? A doctor of laws, arrogant, with a gift for oratory and a wealth of literary resources, that left the fishermen, and Dr. Luke himself, speechless.

For better or worse, Saul became the new number thirteen of the club. With unforeseen artifices and skills.

His story about falling off his horse was unconvincing and lame. What pacific light, what benign tumble? Thrown from his horse without breaking a rib, a leg, an arm, without suffering even a scratch? What kind of fall was that, which only blinded him and covered his eyes with scales? Nothing is said about the horse. Wouldn't it have been spooked, rearing into the air, and galloping away? And the witnesses to the whole thing, silent then and afterwards?

The fishermen's tactic, however, was to embrace everyone. "Whosoever is not against me is for me," the Master had said. Therefore, despite his past and precedents, they welcomed Saul.

After Stephen was no more, someone wise and intelligent like him was needed. Saintliness wasn't all that important and didn't enter into the calculation. Besides which, how could simple fishermen oppose that charismatic figure, who concealed the man of blood, anger, violence and vengeance? His entrance into the club, debated in secret and hurriedly approved without significant opposition, meant prestige as well as insurance against stoning. His life, in the final analysis, would bring the sudden change of a hero who ended up with his head cut off. A small price, by the way, to pay for immortality. Consider: Christ himself had died on a cross between two criminals. Peter also died on a cross, but upside down and without a thief to torment his final moments. Terrible thing to die with an idiot beside you vomiting asininities. John, the virgin, the loved one, who was allowed to rest his head on the Master's chest, had the worst of deaths, the death of lobsters and crabs, thrown into a cauldron of boiling oil. No! From any point of view, the decapitation of Saul was a concession the devil granted to number thirteen. Even from a Roman standpoint, it was worth it. The best death, said Caesar, is a quick one.

Despite everything, giving each his due, Saul's metaphors are unsurpassed, even if from time to time he would assert some nonsense dressed up as eloquence. Such as: "If Christ be not risen, our faith is in vain." Great discovery! Look, Saul, if Christ did not resurrect, everything He said, and you preached, would have a different meaning, and be nothing but a grand hoax and fraud. The fact is that we haven't the slightest evidence that Christ resurrected except through skimpy testimony depending on Faith. Poor Faith. Called into service to bear a burden beyond its strength. Irrefutable witnesses, for example, would have been Annas, Caifás, Pilate, or Herod, if Christ appeared to them in person, taking along as witness Andrew or some relative of his well-qualified to document the fact. Wouldn't it perhaps have been better if the Roman centurion were called to stick his finger into the wounds? Or Barabbas himself? The conversion of Barabbas instead of Saul represented an irrefutable triumph of nascent Christianity. A formal statement by Lazarus, also irrefutable, as well as those He called forth from the dead. As preamble, let them tell us what the realm of darkness was like. What they saw there. It's difficult to understand how Lazarus, intimate friend, who divided with Jerusalem the tears shed by Christ on earth, never opened his mouth to utter the first thing about the One who summoned him from the gates of death. There are such friendships, and, in spite of ourselves, we continue to honor those who most grievously disappointed us in life.

Almost all the testimony that these people, credulous or captious, left us about the resurrection of Christ, put their entire weight on the crutches of Faith. Faith, the Grand Dame destined to become the Muse of Christianity, does not submit to the demands that the times impose on her. She speaks and inspires really anyone, but suddenly abandons her most devout followers and clients, those enraptured ones who bought her enchantments at inflationary prices. Those, she treats like a femme fatale, who takes pleasure in painting the splendors of the few instants she spends with lovers on earth, deluding them with the promise of sempiternal ecstasy in a golden palace, without to the present day ever having given the tiniest demonstration that such a palace exists. An illustrious prostitute, in short, to whom we attribute the purity of angels and the innocence of virgins. Saul, however, introduced a sublime concept into the history of thought when he spoke of the mystical body of Christ. The hymn he raises to

Charity is imbued with lyricism surpassing Solomon and constitutes one of the most beautiful passages in all of literature. "Though I speak with the tongues of men and of angels, and have not charity, I am become as sounding brass, or a tinkling cymbal.... And though I bestow all my goods to feed the poor, and though I give my body to be burned, and have not charity, it profiteth me nothing."

It is sublime. Christ himself could not say it better. There, the mystique of pardon would be learned. For the Jews, the Romans, the Saracens. And the Christian would never clamor for revenge for the barbarity they suffered through the ages because of that Faith and Union in Christ. What the Christian does learn from Christ is to forgive when others strike him in the face, spit on him and nail him to the cross. What the Jews didn't learn from Christ is their "an eye for an eye, a tooth for a tooth." Which, followed to the letter, would end with a world full of the blind and toothless. Not a pleasant sight. In that, Christians rise above mortals. Forgiveness is more incisive than alms in opening the portals of heaven. Saul saw this better than anyone. The most noble virtue in the heart of man is to pardon him who does us wrong.

As for his courage, "*è tutta un'altra facenda*" ["it's a completely different matter"] as the Italians say. How can one conceive of a hero of his stamp and temperament getting into a basket with ropes and descending the walls of Rome to escape the fury of his enemies? Who could imagine Christ, Caesar, Pompey, even Brutus stooping to such? Where was Roman courage? What had he learned from Christ confronting the Jews face to face in the streets, triumphally entering Jerusalem after the epic routing he had dealt the moneychangers in the temple? What had he learned from the "Quo vadis" by which Christ had admonished Peter?

Mud and light, the summation of the ray of illumination that constitutes humanity. No case better illustrates the eternal struggle between Light and Darkness than the life of this hero. And because of this, because it filled the vacuum of endless anxiety in human intelligence, legends and more legends arose creating and shaping beautiful theologies, each more imaginative and intriguing than the last, more elevated and profound, attested to by the formidable beacon of myths. With their prophets, their poets, and their messiahs in attendance. And the indispensable need for a Savior, a Great Messiah. And it is from that demand and in those contingencies that Christ would be born. Sent by the Great Kyrios. Good, Omnipotent, Absolute. To vanquish the Kyrios of Darkness and his demons. To end once and for all the formidable power of the other world and its influence in this one, and to regenerate everything once more. *Ecce nova facio omnia*. Behold that I shall make everything anew. As will say an apocalyptic prophet. A new Heaven and a new Earth. New men, new beasts. New sun, new planets, new solar systems. Implanting a realm of light, of peace, and of love. The coveted Jerusalem. Where men, fishes, and animals will live in peace. Everything returning to the imagined paradise.

Eve continued her ecstasy of visions, as if reading the future in palms. Often, the listeners were unsure what she was saying, but the tale fascinated more for the way it was told than for what it actually said.

And, in those expectations of Faith and Hope, strange and novel concepts, yet indispensable in the new regime, all seeking the good graces of their Kyrios, will offer fattened victims pleasant to the smell, sacrificing cattle, lambs, goats, living humans, all immolated in the flames. Amid prayers and chants of happiness, enraptured people looking heavenward, seeing visions, speaking in tongues. It will be like this in the temples, which they will call churches. Believing in signs in the sky. Falling stars. Tremors in the earth. And priests and prophets to interpret their meaning. Investigators of the mysteries of the shadows, specialists in that which no one sees. Religions will arise, which are vessels that navigate in the shadows with the torches of Faith, under the pretext of seeking the dreamed-of paradise. Churches will spring up on every corner, each clamoring that it alone possesses the route to light. That the others lead only to darkness, with Satan the helmsman. And so, the empresarios of Faith will build industries of fear, and the largest of them, the multinational of consciousness, with its headquarters in Rome, where Peter's successors sit, alternating the throne with moneychangers, the successors of Judas, whose business of selling Christ continues full steam ahead.

Chapter Eleven

All of this, however, began with the desire of Light to solve the mystery of Darkness, and never having succeeded in putting an end to its mysterious and absolute empire. And Darkness mocked everything. Proud of having made the dominant intelligences, adoring them as such, and recognizing them as an untouchable Great Kyrios, immortal and enormous, and the originator of fabulous myths.

For these presentations, the Creator was invited and sat in the chair of honor beside Agapé, his wife, while Eve, with her dramatic and creative talent, noted and detailed everything. She taught Adam the action, the gestures, the way of speaking, the magic that words acquired on stage. In and out of context. Hours went by. She was patient teaching the less gifted animals. The dumbest, apparently, were the crabs, walking backwards when in reality they were walking forward. With which others, not without reason, disagreed. They must have had the concave/convex view of the universe and the rotating movement of the worlds. And the holders of that vision are blessed with great discernment. For the surest way to hit a target is to run away from it in order to attack it from the front. Which distinguishes independent and relative realities in time and space and beyond. The crab sees that advancing forward is to pursue that which is fleeing and technically to lose ground. A fatal error that everyone commits, including male and female movie stars. Each one moving forward, toward nothing, with neither destination nor end.

The Earth, more intelligent, moves one way, and the Moon, even more so, in another, against the Sun. To advance, it's necessary to walk sideways or backwards, the crabs contend, or around themselves, like Brás Cubas. Crab-walking irrefutably delineated the famous theory erroneously known as "relative," when in actuality it is absolute.

The great Einstein could say with assurance that he had graduated from the university of the mangroves.

Our esteemed brother ass would have a lively and singular understanding of what is called inertia. He was devoted to the state of permanence. Permanence preserved things in an immutable, eternal state. In permanence he saw the chief virtue of the Great Kyrios, who left all things the way they were. He spoke so highly of permanence that he enchanted the stars themselves. One statement of his became a classic of equine eloquence. It left the sun speechless and made the stars weep. And he soon came to be considered the Cicero of earthly quadrupeds. The sloth quickly turned into his votary and, with the fervor of a new Christian, climbed trees without ever coming down, to preach the gospel of permanence to the clouds and stars. Such considerations led the ass to profound reflections and to ask himself why the stars didn't fall on his head. On the same day he was taking a nap under a jackfruit tree when a jackfruit almost scrambled his brains, gravity was discovered and he anticipated Newton and Galileo by countless millennia. And founded the school of the stoics, demonstrating by practical example that a blow to the head was as if nothing had happened. Which was to identify him with mystics throughout the ages. This was why he had been honored and chosen by the Great Kyrios to carry into Egypt the new King of the World. For that very reason he was called Zeferino, bearer of the Great Kyrios. The decision left the camel so furious and consumed by envy that it started to buck and explode its anger through deadly outbursts. Finding itself frustrated at having provoked the decapitation of innocent saints.

In fact, since that night in Bethlehem, it had felt scorned and offended by those people who showed their preference for an ass. As it had contacts in Herod's court, it used them to spread the news that the future King of the Jews was hiding among shepherds who planned to flee with Him on the back of a donkey.

Chapter Twelve

It was in the camel's villainy, which was just beginning, that we became aware of the nobleness of soul and the character of the donkey. Truly, few know the history of the one chosen for the solemn entrance of the Messiah into Jerusalem. Zeferino, as we have seen, had been given that name since the journey to Egypt, when he carried on his back Mary and the newborn King of the Jews.... Which left the camel beside himself with anger.

Not without reason. Besides being able to offer a luxurious mount, comparable to a Cadillac nowadays, he stood out as the renowned astronomer of the desert and premier tourist guide of his time, having led, with scientific precision, the Magi from the East to a manger in Bethlehem, guided only by a star. An unprecedented act in the annals of astronomy, which in future centuries would challenge Vasco da Gama, Columbus, and Magellan.

Above all, what made the camel nearly die of envy was that title of "Zeferino," the bearer of Zeus, the thing he most desired in the world. Fearing that the Great Kyrios, by way of compensation, would create the "Constellation of the Donkey" instead of a "Constellation of the Camel." Seven golden stars shining in the heavens, symbolizing the four legs, the head, the tail, and the hump on his back.

He therefore tried every means to defame his nameless rival, hurling every kind of vileness and derogatory epithet. "Midget horse!" "Turd-size!" "Ass!" "Beast!" Who never charged a cent for a trip to the end of the world! (The camel had demanded of the Magi six hundred drachmas per day, in addition to water, food, stabling, and a nighttime companion chosen by him.) "You idiot!" "Jackass!" "Mule!" "Blockhead!" Names that have endured to this day and denote the entire race. Which teaches us a great piece of wisdom: the envious possess surprising and convincing linguistic secrets.

There is no doubt that, because of that august mission, he had been gifted with prophetic vision, trying futilely to emulate the method of his distant cousin, Balaam's donkey, stopping here and there as if an angel were blocking his way. Judas twisting his tail from behind while in front of him the complicitous apostles offered support and laughed.

As steward of the apostles Judas saw, in the solemn entrance of the Messiah, even atop a donkey, a great success that would guarantee an increase of a hundred percent in the collection. What he had pictured was a triumphal entrance in a golden chariot with pearls encrusted in the seats and ivory in the wheels, a silk canopy, rich fluttering garments, a tiara befitting a ruler . . . in the style of the supreme priests who carried the Ark of the Covenant in solemn ceremonies, brilliant white Arabian stallions with silver harnesses—to fix instantly in the minds of the people that Jesus was truly the foretold Great Messiah, come to free Israel from opprobrium and Roman domination. With him on foot at the side, in royal raiment, gaze distant and lofty, receiving in large flagons gold, silver, and precious stones. Fragrances from the Orient.

This grandiose dream of Judas's wilted suddenly, until it transformed into a kiss in Gethsemane. A furtive kiss on the cheek of the Messiah.

The Master had opposed the show of opulence, and the apostles had protested vehemently. "Absolutely not, you lamebrain!" said Peter. "If you go on putting these silly ideas in people's heads, I'll cut off your—" A stern look from the Master made him swallow the swearword. *"Non clericat!"* ["He does not preach!"] said Dr. Luke softly. He had mastered the language of the Romans and imposed an academic authority on the speech of his comrades. They all felt the suggestion from Judas would destroy the image in Isaiah: "my kingdom is not of this world . . ."

Judas twisted his tail, with him refusing to move, trying to deliver a kick to the shin of the rogue, already having missed twice and concentrating on the third. That was when Peter took notice and, seeing the scandal to which they were exposed, with his sharp fisherman's fingernail, gave a furious pinch in the rear end of Zeferino. That son of a mare, accustomed to Peter's pinches, didn't even make an ugly expression. Then the Prince of the Apostles, realizing it, turned to the bearer.

"Stop that, Christopher (Peter sometimes preferred to call him this, believing that Zeferino sounded too pagan), how unseemly. If you want to enter into our service, preach the good news. You have to act like people, be charitable, forgive offenses . . ."

"Forgive my ass! That son of a bitch isn't worth what the cat buries. You bunch of crazies don't see anything wrong with that, haven't any idea what he's planning. In the end, the wretch is going to stretch his neck hanging from a fig tree. Mark my words . . . too late . . . too late . . . But, before that happens—"

He looked surreptitiously to both sides, and—bam!—caught the wretch squarely in the leg. The beast gulped without moving a muscle, without making a face.

Peter and the others were transfixed, not understanding one iota of what was going on, flabbergasted, observing the Master, who watched everything without raising a finger to Judas or giving any indication of reprimanding Zeferino. The animal planted his feet firmly on the ground, and no one could make him budge. Luckily, the young Jewish boys and the people accompanying him noticed nothing and went on shaking the olive branches and singing glorias and hosannas to the Son of David.

The intrepid Zeferino, frustrated and foreseeing all that was about to happen, sought any way possible to prevent the Messiah from entering the city and falling into the hands of the Jews. At some point, seeing that refusing to move was to no avail, lacking the luck of his cousin and without an angel appearing there and expressing itself in Burrese, the rich and florid dialect of burros, raised his face to the sky and emitted several apocalyptic brays, sufficient to alert the Master to the impending tragedy, saying and gesturing that the reprobate who twisted his tail was the same one who would betray him. He showed the sign on his back, indicating the type of death that awaited him. (It is fitting at this point to remember the oracle who for years followed the way of burros, for someday one of them would carry the Great Kyrios to Egypt and another would enter Jerusalem with Him, and thus be granted free admission to heaven.) The Messiah thanked him, smiled with emotion, and said there was no other way, for it was the express will of the Father. He would entreat, weep, and sweat blood, to see if He could be moved to change his mind, but it was so difficult... so difficult.... When the Old One wanted something, it would come about. His bitter destiny and his mission on Earth, in keeping with the role he played in the drama of Scripture. The world was truly not prepared for this, the Son of the Great Kyrios treated like a thief, carrying a cross on his back through half the city. The majority of mankind would never understand, if anyone would ever understand. In any case, it was for this that he had come into the world. He patted Zeferino warmly and caressed his neck. Few witnessed the curious demonstration of affection between the Son of the Great Kyrios and that despised animal. Thus was sealed one of the most sincere friendships in the world.

He accompanied Christ anonymously on the path to Calvary amid the tumultuous crowd delirious at the sight of blood. Some wondered aloud what the ownerless donkey was doing there. It was finally identified by one of the moneychangers whom Jesus had scourged three days earlier. When he saw him, the man roared a guffaw with a mouth of faulty teeth capped with the gold he sold as powder. "Pure gold from Solomon's mines!" he shouted, venturing to show Christ himself the result of the blow.

He raised a tremendous commotion, pointing out to the soldiers the donkey that had carried Christ into Jerusalem. Why not force the would-be King of Israel to haul the cross while riding him? A sublime example of ridicule in the apotheosis of Redemption. Supreme sarcasm that he, however, had been able to present as simulated compassion. For he claimed that Christ was showing signs of not being able to go on and arrive at Calvary alive. The response was a blow of the whip to his mouth. To the delight of the mob, seeing him scramble after the tooth rolling on this ground and several boys in pursuit. It was the second lashing the moneychanger had suffered.

Zeferino, from that moment, seated himself more firmly. Some of the bystanders, moved, ran their hands along his back. He was grateful and from time to time cast a commiserating look at the Messiah, as if to say: "Courage, my friend! Just a little more ... and it will be over ..." Words he would repeat when Christ, in agony, lamented: "Father, Father... why hast Thou abandoned me?!" Zeferino suffered mightily, shaken and sharing the pain.

As a precaution, he moved away and sprawled in the folds of the hillside. He crossed his legs and, unable to bear what he was seeing, closed his eyes and cried bitterly. No one saw him like that. To this day, no artist has glanced at the sublime pietà.

At three o'clock, when darkness fell over the land, his bray was so powerful that the hills shook, giving the impression that he, and not Christ, was delivering his spirit. Before him, sepulchers opened, and the resurrected dead began to emerge from the caves, leaping, dancing, forming a street group, celebrating something they themselves did not understand, called back to life but thinking they were still dead. As if the joy capturing them were a motel at the edge of the highway, where someone spends the night knowing the journey will continue the next day. They celebrated for its own sake, stretching legs numbed by the cave. A sensation both tremendous and strange. Let us remember that we are speaking of outlaws and thieves whose legs were broken to hasten their death and who were entombed in the same common grave of Golgotha. The forces of Justice had united them there. The Great Democratic Justice that unites the just and the unjust. The Justice of intact and broken limbs! On Earth as in Heaven. Amen.

Someone, it is not known who, nor is it of any interest, had remembered to liberate them. It was urgent to flee as soon as possible from that trench, the dark valley of the dead, and everything there, to leave behind the shadows of terror. And they came out running and forming a group of revelers. Quickly, quickly before a malevolent fate called them back.

They commented among themselves the treatment in the

other life. Some had had to eat fingernails. Some, who had no nails, fought over the nails of others. Still others boasted of the vomit they ingested. While certain others insisted they remembered nothing at all.

Tourists, all of them, enjoying an unearned holiday. When they passed the great cross in the middle of Calvary, they were content to learn that the One there was only a political agitator, sorcerer and blasphemer. He had driven into the sea a herd of swine without paying their owner a cent. He had sworn to destroy Solomon's temple and rebuild it in three days; a raving lunatic, stating categorically that He and the Father were One. In the end, he was nothing but a penniless visionary who had managed the incredible feat of angering the doctors of Law, the fanatical patriots, and the Romans all at once, and who had been condemned by Justice the same way he had condemned them. Only a few stopped to contemplate the dour ill-fated colleague. And the rabble catcalled: "Serves you right, Galilean! You're getting what you wanted!"

Indignant at all that, Zeferino held back the tears, and from his corner he opened his mouth and vented: "Scum!!! Scum!!! Scum!!!" No one paid any attention—as who would?—to the imprecations of a crazy ass sitting there bemoaning the loss of his owner. And they went on leaping in that improvised carnival of the dead.

Zeferino, his heart light and contrite, felt a new joy arise in him. Because, in his innermost being he thought the words the Master had just uttered, "Today you will be with me in paradise," were meant for him, only him and no one else.

For these and other reasons, the secret friend of Christ was raised to the category of mystic, admired by a saint who called him brother. He frequented courts, counseled popes, kings and princes throughout the world, assuming now and then the leadership of power either temporarily or permanently. In this way the great geniuses of history, the donkey, the saint, the sloth, and the crab, the precursor of relativism, came together.

Chapter Thirteen

In Eve's theater, everyone collaborated. Each one had a function, a role. Every day, something different. The first auto was the dawn of the world, the creation of the sun and the stars, bursting forth from the darkness as a flower does from the stalk. The most beautiful thing ever seen inside or outside the orb. The sun, the stars, and the darkness insisted on playing themselves. There was a skull fight to see who would play the Great Kyrios. It was called a skull fight because after they died, they still went on battling as if they were alive. Which became a spectacle in its own right, curiously especially at night. The skulls, illuminated and glowing, seemed like fearless warriors pummeling each other, brandishing a femur, a shinbone, or, in desperation, throwing the phalanges from their fingers like bombs. No one could manage to separate them, nor did either succeed in vanquishing the other, all night long. They fought and fought until they fell dead, when there was no longer anyone interested in the outcome. Disconsolate, as if the world had only now ended for them. It's the saddest thing to see a dead and spiritless skull. The fighting didn't appear to be exclusive to the beings of those days. The custom proliferated through the ages. Even today, when one passes a cemetery at night, it's not rare to hear skulls battling, with their colleagues gathered around, egging them on with shouts and taunts. They say it's not just gangs that beat up on one another. In general, all those who feel cheated, or who left behind some greviance in life, roam around there, awaiting the arrival of their enemies, prepared for revenge.

Without a doubt, the most famous in recent history was President Richard Nixon. Standing atop a pile of bones higher than the walls. You couldn't help but envision a Goliath brandishing his grandfather's shinbone, gigantic in stature, massacring, one by one, the reporters and his detractors in life. Phenomenal! And he, who spent a year training for the first waltz, went on stamping out a crazed foxtrot on the head of Eisenhower, who kept screaming, "Stop it, Dick, you son of a bitch!"

On an evening when nothing was scheduled, or at least nothing interesting, there's no greater entertainment than spending a few hours in the cemetery, watching the dead settling accounts with old enemies.

Let's return to the presentations in paradise. The rhinoceros, the hippopotamus, the elephant, the dinosaur, the lion, the camel, principal candidates to play the Great Kyrios, went at it tooth and nail in a bloody trampling and laceration of flesh. It was as if the beginning of the world were starting at its end. It was necessary for Adam to administer some hefty blows with a tree branch, injuring a dozen bystanders in so doing. The dinosaur took such a beating that it limped away dragging one leg and with unsteady hindquarters. In the process, it lost one row of teeth, leaving the other useless. The bloodshed was such that it couldn't even speak. The others took advantage and cut him from the cast. Actually, he didn't possess the slightest talent other than size and strength. Considered by all to be bloodthirsty, rowdy, lacking the refinements of an actor. Much less for the role of the Great Kyrios, coveted by everyone.

In the end, they decided to take a vote. And the elephant won easily. His manners, his impressive trunk, his mystic eyes, and, above all, his transcendental tone of voice gave him the victory without a runoff. The sentimentalists referred to his custom of returning to his place of birth to die. A habit worthy of being emulated. Some of the highly edified claimed they imagined seeing the skulls of David and the prophets walking by themselves to the place where they were born.

The runner-up was the camel. His supporters pointed out his messianic spirit in bearing on his back those who venture into the desert following their star. His detractors spoke of physical deformity, his ill humor and sour smell, his public display of disrespect. Even the donkey garnered a good number of votes. Which led to another show of temper by the dinosaur, who wanted to resume fighting, with the backing of the camel.

The Great Kyrios applauded frenetically the original presentation of the play, proud of witnessing the intelligence of the creatures he had put on Earth. During the act, he whispered to his wife, saying that Eve had forgotten to include the great explosion from the Darkness. No one there really knew how the world had come about.

Chapter Fourteen

In the second auto came the creation of the seas, the fishes, the rivers, the waterfalls. Eve insisted on emphasizing the Amazon, the largest in the world, and Iguaçu Falls, the largest on earth. (Here, Clyto interrupted again to say he couldn't understand why the shark had no role in that play. The earthworm ingeniously replied that they by nature are tragic actors, and tragedy had yet to be invented. He tried to control himself but couldn't.) Begging your pardon, but the version he'd heard since infancy about creation coincided only up to a certain point with hers, but afterwards no. True, in the beginning, everything was darkness that dominated infinite space. Yes, that Darkness was made up of dense clouds of black resembling an extremely fine liquid that was the condensation of everything.

Then came forth the great shark swimming in the darkness. Flying, for his fins were wings, and not even the seas existed yet. Quickly recognized and adored as a powerful kyrios from another sphere, another world, wise and absolute lord. And he didn't want to be alone, so he created a wife, in his image and likeness. And from them came the first shark couple, in the model that exists today. And he said, "Be fruitful and multiply. It is written: 'Let there be no virgins among you.' Virginity is cursed ignominy. The Virgin, the chaste, is someone who has chosen, temporarily or not, to undermine the fertility and the force of renewal of the species. The perverse homo goes beyond that and says in the face of the Creator, 'Fok that business of children! I don't want to reproduce!' It's as if he chanted the song: *I want to come / With another man / Who pleasures me without getting tired* . . . And shouted with his arms raised, Viva Sodom! Viva Gomorrah! Viva the Isle of Lesbos! Death to Moses and the priests of the Inquisition!

And the hedonist, shamelessly ejaculating, becomes the terror of sperm. "Pleasure! Pleasure! Fok that business of babies!"

"I'll kill anyone who shows up here with a penchant for being a eunuch!" the Kyrios of the sharks thundered from the darkness. "Anyone sterile will be burned like a stick of wood. 'A fig tree that bears no fruit becomes firewood.'" After which, seas, rivers, lakes, even watering holes, brimmed with fishes large, medium, and small according to their species. As things should be.

He recalled that, as a youngster he had often heard of the Amazon, and even now the grandfather sharks related to their little grandchildren sharks the grandeur of the ocean-river, the apotheosis of waters, whose currents sweep away entire islands, without mixing with the salty sea, elevating to the heavens the legendary pororoca, the greatest spectacle on earth, to which nothing can compare. Also among its marvels is the vitória-régia, a waterlily capable of bearing the weight of a couple courting on it.

The shark then excused himself, with a polite gesture for Monice to continue.

Expressing her gratitude wide-eyed, with a small laugh and a toss of her head, she did so.

"After conquering drama, Eve turned to comedy. She chose the creation of woman and man. Again, success was instantaneous. Agapé, setting aside her customary manners, doubled over in hysterical laughter, becoming purple, blue, and scarlet, accompanied by convulsions. The Creator, in turn, laughed from beginning to end. He laughed, doubled over, so much that he got a bellyache again, and a kink in the colon. Someone thought to bring him wormwood and anis to chew. A miraculous remedy till then unknown to him. That was when he remembered to create Pharmaceutical Science. Explaining what herb should be good for what and when. And he placed in charge of the new science a young angel without wings—there were very few in those days—called Emmanuel, the future Jesus. He became passionate about Medicine, which he elevated to the category of science with his ability and his genius. He invented the art of performing miracles. First transforming water into wine. Later, multiplying bread and fish. He walked on water and calmed the storm. He cured lepers with a mere touch of his hand. Cured the blind using mud and spit. The lame, cripples and the paralyzed—everything as if were child's play that the other angels couldn't duplicate. His art reached the height of sublimity, but people thought he had lost his senses when he began expelling demons and bringing back the long-dead.

Thus was the first doctor in history. However, since there were so many to be treated, he recruited assistants and chose wasps, the patron saints of the sick, and the venomous serpent, patroness of doctors.

Other assistants included the dog, the cat, and ants. In this way, medical science came to be the bailiwick of good hands, good bites, and good tongues.

Chapter Fifteen

It is good to remember that, *ab origine*, it was man who came from woman and not woman from man. (The shark gulped at that moment, opening his serrated mouth to voice a rebuttal but reluctantly restrained himself, fearful of ruining the amorous conquest he felt was certain.) The Creator (explained Eve in a lively demonstration of her magnificent power of expression, using her eyes, shaking her head, the seemingly unrehearsed tossing back of her hair, which fell onto her suntanned forehead, her fingers busily pouring forth images), having created everything, took on the task of making woman from the clay of the ground. But that decision came only after much reflection. He had first imagined making her of salt; later, he thought she would be beautiful in stone, alabaster, onyx, or marble from Atlantis. Better, perhaps, from a living plant, like the trunk of a palm, the aroma of a cherry tree, or the tropical orchid. He thought and thought and thought, scratching his head, slowly discerning the flower that would become the queen of all flowers, which he would call the rose. He then created the first rose. And little by little, by joining and separating its petals, he formed the calyx, bringing together stamen and pistil and designing the woman. He wasn't very pleased. He redid everything. From back to front, from top to bottom. From the inside out. He experimented with color, the feel of the petals, creating the tube, the limbus, the fauces of the corolla. In this way, came about the lily, the carnation, the dahlia, the magnolia, the luxurious orchid, and thousands of flowers, the most beautiful and the less beautiful, lost to memory and time. All flowers went through that divine experiment. Even the marigold was an intermediate stage of the rose in the pre-creation of woman. All were first drafts either approved or simply rejected prior to the rose, before it was a rose, a mere rough draft of woman.

Once the idea was conceived, the materials were lacking for a living, perfect flower. He considered salt once again and rejected the salty essence. Woman of salt... woman of salt... No, water will dissolve her. Dogs will lick her. The dog is an animal that can't control itself when faced with those things. So, he obsessed about gold all night. Then he became attracted to silver. But on other nights he wavered between emerald and turquoise, between turquoise and rubies. A woman made of rubies! A woman made of rubies! He clicked his tongue. "How beautiful she must be!" He thought about diamond, and the sense of dizziness increased, because what came to mind was the stuff of stars. The idea was so brilliant he leapt and almost twisted an ankle. But he put aside everything he had pondered till then. He thought a woman of star stuff, of diamond, gold, emerald, or ruby would turn out too proud, too vain. Bold in the extreme. Truly unbearable. Hated in the world where she was queen. No one would dare to get close to her. That was when he bent down, spat on the ground, and began to mold the dust of the earth. It was a fine, porous clay, reddish and humid, that takes a long time to dry. Like any artist, he grew enthusiastic about what he was creating. He went into a trance when he created the eyes and the nose. He whistled, a sound resembling the chords of a harp. The warbling of a dove.

He took two rose petals and moved them up, then down, sideways, forming a pleasing shape. The Kyrios was so satisfied with his invention that, later, he would replicate it in producing the nymph, the small seductive labia minora of the vulva. Then he bent down and blew in order to infuse in it the perfume and sweetness of the rose. And thus he gave the first kiss completely raptured by the lips that quivered and wished to bite his own. Be it noted that this was the first amorous interaction of the creature with its Creator. The first seed of love on Earth had been planted, the beautiful tree that would never cease to give fruit and flourish.

The good Kyrios now began to imagine the woman lying down, standing up, walking, rolling her hips in a rhythm that poets alone could describe. She had to be different from the earthworm, or even from the vain serpent admired for her sway, her skill, her fine words, her astuteness, more malicious than any other animal on Earth.

Then there came into his mind the bud of the rose, or more precisely, of the dahlia or the camellia. It was in so doing that he conceived of breasts. The maximum symbol of feminine seduction with which women would hypnotize men eternally in loveplay. It's necessary to understand, interrupted the earthworm with rare emphasis and erudition, that the seductive instinct is inherent and wanders through the silence of the body and belongs to the very essence of the woman. Sleeping or awake, she possesses it, thinking or not thinking, using it or not, nor her first whimper, from the first suckle, when she cries, when she crawls and begins to walk, and grows and becomes what she is, unknowingly, without realizing why or for what. That deceptive mystery inside and outside of herself.

It is spread throughout her skin, speaking a thousand invisible languages that never stop talking. It is in her locks of hair, her eyes, the color of her skin, the softness of her face, the ellipsis of her nose. In the curve of her lips, her entire mouth, her every gesture, in the enchantment of her movements. It is in her navel, in the design, feel and form of her legs, in her foot, in her toes. There were kyrioses who killed themselves over a heel. Even today there are men who duel because of a simple lock of hair. Who flay one another for a toenail.

In no other part does seduction appear as it does in the breasts, for it was there that the Creator sublimated all the sensuality of woman. It is what makes the man awaken desire, admire how lovely the thing is, and witness the birth of an unbearable urge to bite it. She needs that mechanism because she was not equipped like the earthworm or even her serpent cousin. Which, lacking that pretext nevertheless achieve the same effect. However, a women without any of that, with no breasts, no lips, no eyes, without hair or a lyrical sway of the waist, the total seduction of the body, what difference is there between the woman and dry straw?

The earthworm appeared more vain and prouder than ever. She licked her lips with tremendous satisfaction and the coquettishness of a young girl admiring herself in the mirror.

After finishing the breast, the Great Kyrios looked, startled, looked again, proud of himself, enraptured, admiring his work and seeing it was good, it was sublime, beyond any doubt, there was nothing that could compare to it.

Next, he paused again and reflected. It must be understood that these reflections took days and weeks, even entire years. He spent a century delineating the form of the hips. Five years for the nose, a millennium for the entire mouth. And this was after having created the animals. Now, chin in hand, he extended a finger and rubbed his lip. And saw before him, like a beautiful fountain, the tiny mouth of the rose. The navel was born. Which was a dry fount in the preconception of another, beyond. Afterward, he walked back and forth, spun on one foot, bent his heel. The idea turned in his mind like a cyclone, a leaf in the wind. Sometimes, ideas seemed to elude the Great Kyrios, as if he were "it" and playing hide-and-seek. Or some other children's game. He conceived and unconceived. The idea coming and going, with Him coaxing it, then letting go, and it returning to be coaxed anew. He would conceive clearly and then obscurely, the visual effect, angle, contrast, restyling of the profile. All these habits would be copied by the surrealist painters, by Picasso and Dalí. And Cícero Dias. It's said that the last-named whistled even while asleep. He knew about this and did it on purpose, wishing to be admired and remembered among artists. Imitated by painters of genius. Whether in the way he rubbed his nose, whistled, or scratched his head, he wanted to see himself in all of them, even in the uninspired poets and the club-handed scribes.

In this point, the Kyrios seemed prideful and vain. If, when we reach a certain age, we start to lose our intellect, to speak and act stupidly, what can be said about one who has existed forever? There the Creator was. A bit frivolous, albeit majestic and dignified. Beneath the fig tree, in the midday sun. Lying on his back, head on his crossed hands, supported by a rock. One leg raised above the other. His gaze fixed on the horizon, thinking. Actually, he didn't seem like the Almighty. He wasn't paunchy, and surely never would be, even if the hint of a bay window was beginning to show. At his beckoning, an ant brought a leaf for him to chew, which had the same effect as a good glass of wine.

Now, he hesitated over what to do with the sexual organs,

where he wanted to implant mystery, enchantment, the why of everything in nature and in woman. In some animals, he had left the organs exposed; in others, internal and inconspicuous. In some, protected by a padding of skin, in still others, without any protection at all. Finally, unable to arrive at a suitable conclusion, he opted for a temporary solution. "Well, why not?" he said, with a curt, disillusioned grunt followed by a click of the tongue, a longstanding habit, when a fruitful idea occurred to him. And he gave the woman both, exposed and beautiful, like the pistil of a flower.

Undeniable that, in aspect and everything, it was a work of the finest conception. The Great Kyrios had outdone himself. Because it was like a seed, capable of opening into thousands of Eves and thousands of Adams.

In that first-stage plan, the woman would fertilize herself. That is, she carried in herself the male organ with which to produce the man and her own self, in a single act of love. The penis curved downward and met the vulva, which it penetrated to inject the liquid into itself without major complications. The birth infallibly yielded triplets. Three males, three females, or two of one and one of the other, every time. A natural and necessary process to accelerate the propagation of the species.

The man, therefore, came from within her, hidden in a seed, as an integral part of herself, like the heart, the eyes, the breasts. Something no kyrios had ever thought, much less found a way of achieving. With the creation of complete sex in the woman, the Great Kyrios finished the masterpiece of creation.

There would be men, said the earthworm after a brief reflection, who would inherit in their genes the memory of that instant and would never forgive the change. That temporary phase, however brief, was just an interlude with the idea of perfecting the concept before finalizing the work. As in everything, the Creator tried several forms before settling on one he liked. Before arriving at perfection. This explains, for instance, the various feline types that preceded the lion, the various insects that came before the honeybee, the various types of flowers prior to the rose. And, among those various types, the infinite variation.

With implacable and incoherent envy of woman, men would do anything to supplant her. Adopting, in a symbolic transvestism, her physical and psychological constitution. Truly loving one another, marrying, making love. They spend their lives aspiring and contemplating in themselves the mirage of womanhood. "How sublime it would be to put into practice the creator's original idea of self-fertilization!" they think, dreaming and in a state of delirium. To eliminate the need for her, the perennial rival with her enviable constitution, divine, different, and unique. Giving no thought to the paradox, the ridiculousness of the undertaking. Without the natural instruments of mating and fulfillment. After all, where were the divine breasts, the roseate golden vulva, the waist swaying to the lyrical undulation of the hips, which mark the orchestration? The thousand and one hidden tongues that spoke on the surface of the skin? But they would insist on stealing all of that for themselves, even if just the feeling, and, in desire, the same rights, the same privileges, the same fantasies that only the mechanism of woman can produce. They desired to complete each other, so that nature might take a blind frustrated leap to reach the other side. Falling into despair, a psychic and mortal abyss. Such men existed then and would always exist, experiencing in their flesh the drama of ambivalence, criticizing the grave mistake of the One who created them. Because in actuality there are discontents, inside and outside their skin, some rejected in flesh and mind the creative process, some atrophied in sex and love. Perhaps through no fault of theirs. Absolutely none. For they were born that way, and sooner or later they would bend in that direction. Except when they did not. Condemnable such incidents because, no matter how much in vogue, they revile and corrupt the dignity of sex in man and woman by deviating from fertile Nature in purpose, method, and procedure. Men-woman. Women-man. What an abstruse anomaly slipped through the Creator's hands! However, the tragedy perpetuates itself. Beautiful woman imprisoned in the bodies of men. Handsome men chained in the bodies of women. The Creator should be ashamed and publicly renounce the great gaffe he perpetrated.

The earthworm continued to demonstrate her mastery of the topic of biopsychology:

To emphasize everything and underscore beauty, it was necessary to darken the image, to give it dusk, a chiaroscuro in the curves. So, he created hair that tumbled past the navel, falling over the lovely circular fount smiling in the middle of the nave like the corolla of a flower.

Woman was created still sleeping in the clay, her breasts pointing skyward, drying in the sun. He had designed them with total affection and fondness. He had spent an entire millennium on the project. A female monkey passing by was surprised, scratched her own chest, whistled, but left in silence with a self-admiring step, forcing herself to swallow the bitter taste of envy. Agapé, however, upon seeing her, sneaked up on the Great Kyrios, lovingly pulled his ears and said, "Listen, my Old Man, stop being so presumptuous. That there isn't as original as you think. Unconsciously, all you did was reproduce a pallid image of the model that won't leave your head, right? You made an elegant gesture and a quick-step back and forth. You started to find fault with the private parts, the entirety, the angularity. This is missing, that's too much, here, there, everywhere. It'd be better this way; it'd be better some other way." And speaking, talking, and gesticulating, she opened her fine vestments of transparent weave and showed him what the original breasts were like, the fountain of damp lips, half-open, that Aphrodite so many times tried to take, and she, to safeguard her patent of originality, forced the Creator to cover the fount of woman with tender down and give it the triangular shape that has been conserved to the present day. After which, Agapé whirled on her irresistibly sensual alabaster legs.

He said, enraptured, "You're right! You're right! Fruitful love!" The kiss they then exchanged lasted sunsets and mornings without end, to the frenetic applause of the stars and the clamor of the animals of Earth. The woman still dreamed. Anathema to the painters of genius, who neglected one of the most sublime moments of conceptual art: the kiss of Adonis and the dreaming woman.

Chapter Sixteen

There are several versions of how the Great Kyrios created man, one of which is that He yanked the penis from the woman's vulva. That fabulous and brutal dog of paradise, fighting with his companion, lay angry in a corner. Disconsolate and sad, after three days without eating, on the fourth day he went outside and ran into the woman, made of clay by the Great Kyrios and left to dry in the sun. Seeing this, he lost control, bit down on the woman and scurried away with her in his mouth. Unable to keep up with the running dog, the Great Kyrios jumped but misjudged the distance and the only part of the woman that survived was the bloody penis in his hands. He was inspired and smiled, proclaiming to the four corners of the world: "Let there be man!" And thus appeared the king of creation.

For a long time, this version. which the historian/philosophers Zildenstein and Juracyvish discovered in some dusty tome of myths, was in vogue.

Another account they found held that man hadn't been created by the Great Kyrios but by Agapé, his wife. Jealous of the woman and seeing in her a powerful and mysterious rival, with that penis planted in the uppermost part of the vulva, who didn't know what it was or what it was good for. At the time, it seemed to her like a serpent, a scorpion ready to strike, or some astute and malicious instrument that the woman could make use of at any time to supplant her in the art of lovemaking. So, she yanked it out, intending to feed it to the dogs. However, the penis immediately began to grow and grow in her hands and quickly became a man, slender, handsome, and muscular. Affectionate and kind at woman's side.

Startled by the presence of the man, whose image seemed to be equal to that of her Kyrios, she began to want him, to envy him, as if he were a part of him rather than part of the woman. She hid him in the forest, visiting him secretly. One day, the Great Kyrios surprised her and asked:

"Where are you coming from?"

"From the bath," she said.

He, sensing she was lying, went into the forest and discovered the naked man, sitting on a rock in the middle of the spring. Concluding he was her lover and a budding rival. he threw him to the ground amidst the animals. Agapé, acting from vengeance, did the same with the woman.

The reason why to this very day, no man tolerates seeing another male with his woman, and no woman can stand for another female to be with her man. This probable origin of mankind has remained intact for millennia, despite competent historians disagreeing and classifying it as a legend for not conforming to the facts. Now, as we know, fact and legend have been at loggerheads since time immemorial. But in such an important matter, who is going to rule in favor of the facts?

It is necessary to remember, however, that in his youth, the Great Kyrios had been the acknowledged champion of the stellar marathon. A track comprising a billion stars, jumping from one to the next without stopping. He had won brilliantly, leaving the other kyrioses light-years behind. Jupiter, the most arrogant and presumptuous, feared because of his deadly lightning bolts, finished an inglorious second. Uranus, who made all the gold and precious metals in the universe, and because of which everyone was rooting for, came in a distant and humiliating third. Saturn, the gloomiest of the runners, unpredictable, irascible, was what we here call a "dark horse." Without being the favorite, he would sprint at the end and win the race against all expectations. Even so, he ended up in fourth place, panting from exhaustion. Neptune, grandson of a kyrios who devoured his enemies and therefore people feared being eaten alive if he didn't win, unwittingly invented nepotism. Jeered when he came in fifth, his lungs practically hanging out of his mouth. Vulcan, feared for his fire and violence, took sixth place. Right behind, Pluto, who wasn't recognized, perhaps because he was too small, a dwarf next to the others. In addition, they failed to register his name. Besides these, there were others, dozens of kyrioses from all over, from the Orient, the far North, the southern pole, not counting the traditional competitors from the Upper Nile.

Before the race there was a parade in which the contestants distinguished themselves with regional dances and acrobatics. Capoeira, a choreographed game of feline origin that concealed the intention of a treacherous attack and a deceptive defense, was exhibited for the first time.

All those aged kyrioses lived in gilded palaces in the seven points of the orb. The majority of them are gone now, no one knows how or why—perhaps one of those secular epidemics that decimate entire races. Today, they are forgotten in the mists of time. It's said that Jupiter and his court never really died and will one day return to claim his throne as the King of classical mythology, the leading religion of those days.

The Great Kyrios, the champion of a different mythology, had been decorated with a star on his chest and the choice of the most beautiful woman. Adone, his twin sister unknown to Him but known to her, separated from the time they were infants, kidnaped by Jupiter while still a young girl, whose name meant "maximum pleasure." When they married, the Great Kyrios, following ancient custom, gave her the name Agapé, which means "sublime love." None of that is easy to recognize. Jupiter courted Adone since childhood. The Great Kyrios also desired her since childhood, when a simple exchange of glances ignited love in them both.

At the moment of the awarding of the trophy, an indignant Jupiter advanced fiercely upon his rival, tooth and nail. They waged battle like dinosaurs. Blows, capoeira moves, and martial tactics, popular among the kyrioses of the Upper Nile. It was the greatest tumult in the sky since the dawn of time, in a tradition of famous centaurs who fought to the death when a female centaur couldn't decide between them. According to the rules, no one could escape alive. Any disputant who chanced to survive should kill himself, his hoof on the body of the rival, after receiving the coveted trophy of kisses from the lips of the beloved. Then, she too would kill herself. This was followed by a posthumous marriage ceremony, more solemn and pompous than marriage among the living, with the king and queen in attendance and the entire country celebrating. The couple was carried in triumph through the streets. The celebration lasted days. After which, while the vanquished centaur burned in a bonfire, the fortunate couple were buried standing up in a shared grave, above which were erected monuments to the posterity that would transform their love into legend.

Everyone was alarmed, afraid something similar might occur. Then Agapé appeared, in a black wedding gown and carrying a dagger against her naked breast. "She would kill herself then and there, unless the fighting stopped." Jupiter, already on the ground, out of breath, not moving because of the stranglehold he had suffered, finally gave up. They made peace, or, more accurately, arrived at an armistice. The territory would be divided, each with its own beliefs and traditions. Jupiter took possession of classical mythology, while the Great Kyrios was acclaimed the Almighty Lord of the Bible.

Jupiter. however, swore that someday he would take Adone back. So, they went on inflicting wars and damage on each other. And what appeared on the surface to be mere accidents was in reality the fury of those two rolling around the world. According to experts, the disappearance of Atlantis, the destruction of Sodom and Gomorrah, the flood, the Tower of Babel, the eruptions of Vesuvius obliterating Pompeii and Herculaneum, the Black Death, the Lisbon earthquake—in short, all the ills that beset humanity are nothing more than the vengeance of those giants, who because of a woman tear each other apart in a struggle to the death.

Chapter Seventeen

The auto was over, the curtain had fallen. Despite earlier stomach pains, the Great Kyrios applauded the perfection of the comedy/drama, the unique art of the actors, principally the earthworm in the role of Eve, Adam in his, the elephant in the role of the Great Kyrios, a cat who played Agapé, the dog who played himself, much envied because he received more applause than the rest. The Great Kyrios, at Agapé's side, the prototype of Eve, whom he embraced and kissed for having conceived such a lively and intense drama.

Chapter Eighteen

Every afternoon, we attended a different outdoor staging. Alternating between drama and comedy. It came to the point where people demanded something spicier and insisted that Eve give us a tragedy. She demurred, saying that tragedy was by nature a hazardous genre, risky and violent, with unpredictable psychological repercussions. Furthermore, there was no appropriate theme, for the time being, nor actors trained for it. They insisted so much, so much that she ended up yielding and, little by little, formed an idea. But she still didn't know how to shape it into dialogues and scenes, nor even what materials she needed.

Chapter Nineteen

A blazing hot summer night. Eve was sweating buckets, exhausted, when she finished relating the story of the bad angels who rebelled and were cast into the abyss. The children were sleeping. Contrary to what was expected, there was no customary burst of applause. Everyone was contrite, fearful, lacking the courage to meet the gaze of the Great Kyrios. A mortal menace hovered over their heads. In their minds, the curtain had not yet fallen. The Great Kyrios himself and Agapé were late in hugging Eve. Yes, they praised the play, but in a cool and distant way. They measured for the first time the extent of the woman's genius. They were nonplused to see their secrets exposed on stage. Because everything that purported to be pure imagination had actually occurred in some form, or would occur, in other circumstances, proportion, and setting. It was necessary to pay attention to the woman's intuition and abilities. She was capable of imagining heavens, hells, and the myths that created them. Of populating them with kyrioses and demons that pummeled one another to death. And to make them seem real. Her creatures were impressionable and, in general, highly believable. In subsequent tragedies, Eve must consult with Him beforehand and detail the plot and the context. "It's dangerous," he thought, "with her resources the woman can become a type of bad angel among us."

All of it, however, as impressive as it was, had merely been pure imagination on the part of Eve. As has already been said, she related her stories orally before putting them on stage. It depended on a successful reception from the audience. She was convinced it would never reach the stage. She needed to change so much that it would be simpler to invent another. A real tragedy, gripping, the kind they were asking for. That is, human, universal. Few of those there were concerned with the fate of angels, whose presence among them was only shadow and fantasy, inconstant voices lost amid the lashing of waves and the chorus of winds. At the same time, Eve, seeing that the rebellion of the angels had left a negative impression on the Creator and apprehension in his creatures, wished to recover from the fiasco as quickly as possible. By focusing on the power and majesty of the Great Kyrios, Lord of the Universe, and the condition of his creatures, as humble and obedient children who depended on Him for everything. Far from easy, however, to design something like that. She spent days on end thinking and choosing before a theme occurred that pleased her. And was convincing.

A certain premonition began to plague her from the moment the idea appeared. She was unable to come to a satisfactory decision. She couldn't see clearly either the script or the Creator's reactions. She first consulted with Adam, who found the plot fabulous. Excellent, in fact, even if it was risky and subject to misinterpretation. She would have to work more on the phrasing, details, the conveyors of the final impression, taking into account the several levels of the audience's comprehension. And think about how the Great Kyrios and Agapé would receive it, think about the kyrioses on Olympus who wanted to be included, knowing of their involvement in recent dramas. Should she invite Beelzebub, the supreme Kyrios of the Upper Nile, for the same reason? These parties would surely be the most difficult to satisfy. In contrast to the animals, who explored the comical side of the play and were only interested in evoking laughter. The humans, above all, who didn't understand themselves, ignoring past and future, were more worried than anyone.

Eve shook her head. In a certain way, she and Adam felt the final impression would never be erased from their minds, forcing them to relive the drama/tragedy in flesh and blood for the rest of their lives. Especially Cain, married to his sister, perpetually ill-humored but possessing a clear intelligence and unmatched good sense, who criticized everything, malicious, suspicious, rowdy. She must make it clear that rebellion against the Great Kyrios was an unforgivable crime punishable by death, which is to say total paralysis of the senses. Without explaining exactly why. She had even come to think that sleep was some mysterious kyrios who took them away each night to regions they would someday inhabit. They died at night, so to speak, but lived again when they awoke. Mysterious sleep, one of the most intelligent things the Creator had done. Another would be the awareness of the world around her. Using it, she racked her brain long into the night. And He, seeing her, never explained anything.

The final impression, Adam said, was good, although it should create anticipation, suspense. More symbols, some enigmatic, some explicit, keeping pace with the plot, beginning to end. Eve agreed. After some discussion about casting, what level of language to use, length, and scenery, both were certain that with this play she would redeem herself before Him. Without telling the actors how the end would be, she decided to bring to the stage what would come to be known in history as "the Temptation of Eve" and "the episode of the apple."

She revised, changed everything from start to finish, applying the last retouches to the parts, uniting everything in the script with the logic to which each image, each word, each comma must obey. She tested everything using several approaches, the various moods that assaulted her day by day.

She handed out the roles. The snake would play herself. As would Adam. The setting would be the central square of paradise with a tree at its center. For the role of Eve, she had chosen the earthworm, a gifted actor, versatile, the most talented and competent of the cast. In the final reading, she had competed with the serpent and won unanimously with the judging panel, headed by the giraffe, who was dissatisfied and grumbled she was being discriminated against because of her height and "excluded from all the roles." The chameleon, the lizard, the viper, more than anyone the serpent, who gnashed her teeth from envy, curling up in a corner, sticking out her tongue whenever she saw the earthworm. Waving her rattle in her face. The earthworm pretended not to notice, bearing it all with patience, dignity, and the class demanded by the role, living the drama and embodying the temperament and manners of the person she was playing, even offstage. "Noblesse oblige," the norm of behavior she adopted long before the French discovered it. Delicate observers of good taste, they copied, to the letter, our gestures and customs, propagating them in Europe and courts around the world.

You will be cursed among all animals! "In your blindness, I shall crush your head if you try to bite my heel," said, in a single voice, the chorus of worms, who had remained in a corner of the stage, garbed in black, white hat, and small silk tie, expressing the sentiments that the charismatic virgin represented, placing a foot on the serpent. Later, theologians would attribute novel concepts to the mind of the Creator. An immaculate birth without penetration! Perhaps inspired by Oriental myths.

Precisely because of this curse in the end, the serpent went around dying of rage, bitter over her fate, shaking at the mere thought. Seeing herself beaten and crushed by "that shitty earthworm," even if it wasn't true. "Damn it! What luck I have! I denounce you, you cursed thing!!!"

The serpent then began spreading gossip. She started a relentless campaign, spreading the idea that only Eve should play herself. That the most important role couldn't be left in the hands of an imbecile like the earthworm. At a minimum, she lacked the stature required to confront Adam. The earthworm replied instantly that what makes an actor is talent and the art of creating an illusion, by identifying himself with the character being played. By making the audience laugh, cry, feel emotion. To provoke an emotional catharsis is the goal of drama. It has nothing to do with physical stature.

And she referred to a recent drama put on by the ants, staged with the greatest success, involving an impoverished giant from unknown lands, who came to steal the world by carrying it away on his shoulders. With herculean steps, breaking down ancient walls, toppling sacred temples, ruining statues and monuments to ancient heroes and kyrioses, crossing mountains and rivers, impassive to the stones and arrows hurled at him, without anyone feeling the least lack of a real giant onstage.

The serpent was burned up, twisting her tail and wrapping herself around a tree over the naturalness of the earthworm. Her fury was so great that she strangled the fig tree.

Eve remained firm in her refusal to play herself. After all, it was the first tragedy with acts ever staged in the world, and dealing with eternal esoterica, a very difficult task, it demanded someone to oversee the undertaking, handle the parts, serve as prompter to the players, and lead the play from beginning to end. In truth, she was again risking all the prestige hitherto garnered. Moreover, her vision, her philosophy of life, with no certainty of how the Great Kyrios might interpret it. She was not going to consult him, despite everything. She wanted it to be a surprise, during the drama. Notwithstanding the initial admonition he had given her, she decided to proceed. She would keep him in suspense, enraptured from the opening to the closing curtain. The finale crowns the work. Adam agreed. "Risky and intriguing, yes. But no important work is done without tearing down taboos about orders of evidence and common sense. To the stage, my sapodilla!" It was the last time he would call her that.

They remembered that the earthworm had shown incomparable talent, bringing to the stage the first night of love between man and woman. It made her a star. Even the Kyrios couldn't hold back, beside himself with joy. Enchanted, he had gone to Eve and said, "That girl is a prodigy. In the final scene, you could picture Adam rolling in bed with you."

Everything was at the ready. The Tree of the Knowledge of Good and Evil was depicted. Placed somewhere in the center of paradise. No one knew what the tree was. They did know, however, that the Great Kyrios had hidden the seed of all creation in a place no one imagined. A minuscule seed, smaller than a grain of mustard. Eve, with her astuteness, one day discovered where the seed was, stored behind seven keys that He kept on a chain on his waist. It was as if it were a microcosm, a word she had sometimes heard, but only now understood, the condensation of everything created. With it, He would rebuild the world, if necessary. He had to be careful. He knew of the acts of sabotage that Jupiter was constantly preparing, and of that brother of his from the darkness, the barbaric, unpredictable Beelzebub. Every day, he observed black clouds building in the distance, covering the silvery peaks of the Upper Nile, where his palace stood and where furious lightning bolts shredded the sky and made the Earth tremble. More enlightened people understood it to be merely storms and hurricanes. Still, prophets and the common folk suspected they were witnessing the pyrotechnic show of the immortal Kyrioses. Let them believe. Remain in a tranquil ignorance, or wisdom, without great consequence for anyone. Even so, the Great Kyrios nurtured concerns that Eve herself didn't understand.

The magic seed was called of good and evil. Because it contained in itself the genes of good with the power to create and recreate everything again and, at the same time, the genes of evil, which would suddenly destroy everything. Therefore, He insisted on keeping the seed in a place totally inaccessible and unimaginable, for He loved the world and its creatures. He knew it would be the end of everything if it fell into the hands of his enemies.

One day, the Great Kyrios was napping in the shade of his favorite fig tree, in the torpor of midday, after some swigs of strong, crisp genipap wine. He adored that wine, perfect for restorative sleep, especially prepared by Eve with second and third intentions. She approached stealthily and removed the key from among the many hanging at his waist, which He loosened when sleeping, leaving them on the ground. And she stole the seed. Yes, stole, but in another sense and with the best of intentions. For the purpose she had in mind. It wasn't theft in the moral and legal sense, but rather a borrowing with the intention of creating suspense in her drama. She would put it back there later. "The finale crowns the work," she thought. A principle that would become a motto in the writing of Machiavelli.

The Great Kyrios told Adam, upon awarding him paradise: "You may eat of all the fruits of paradise, save that of the tree of good and evil. For the day you eat of it, you will feel like Kyrios, equal to Us . . ." That "Us" referred to himself and Agapé. Eve explained this, like everything else, with emphasis and care for the slightest details, lest there be some mistake or false interpretation. There were people there of limited understanding, while others would maliciously miss no opportunity to downplay the theme, foment confusion, and accuse others while feigning innocence. Now, the apple was not supposed to be a real apple. because that way it would lose the desired dramatic effect. It was only an apple seed. A symbol. The seed of "good and evil," of which everyone spoke but no one had ever seen, as she explained. A psychological farse, the kind the Great Kyrios enjoyed. She never had in mind putting on stage a scene of formal disobedience as such, but rather as an act of deserved punishment, something so malevolent that everyone would disapprove when they saw it. Much less did she plan to insult and provoke Him publicly, the Father, all Benevolent and Wise, the omnipotent Kyrios of the world. Who would be foolish enough to dare? Who?

Besides which, Eve was a monarchist by temperament and conviction. From time to time, she would have illusions and dream of one day being a queen, someone with whom the Great Kyrios would suddenly fall in love and fill the world with sons. All of them princes and heirs to the treasures of heaven. Without clarifying the fate of Adam and Agapé, their love companions. Better that way. They were circumspect dreams that left everything as it was found. A dream, just a dream, without entailing consequences in anyone's life.

No, she would never approve of the tactics of the French Revolution or the American Masons, much less the plotting of the serpent. The tree of good and evil, which didn't appear, and therefore didn't exist in the play, planted there in the center of paradise, was pure symbolism.

She had designed a drama with high tension, which would satisfy the various people, the Great Kyrios, men and animals, at several levels of sense and understanding. Eve spent day after day explaining to each actor his or her part, without disclosing to anyone the secret of the ending.

It was this: the serpent would bring the seed in her mouth and present it to Eve (the earthworm), seducing her to eat it, "for on the day you do, you will become full of power and wisdom, with knowledge of good and evil, capable of creating heavens for those you love, and hells for those you hate, immense riches, treasures beyond compare, luxurious palaces, a blissful eternity, at your whim, without having to answer to anyone, as powerful as the Kyrios who created you." The earthworm, after much hesitation and evasion, irresolute and reluctant, took the seed and fearfully raised it to her mouth. The seed, however, fell to the ground. A wind swept it to the center of paradise. And, suddenly, the apple tree was weighted down with beautiful apples. The earthworm couldn't resist. She bit into one. She turned into a Kyria and queen. Beautiful, rich, powerful, intelligent, the envy of the world. And all saw and marveled at that transformation. She began to fear her own metamorphosis. She didn't want to be so beautiful, and rich, and powerful, and intelligent all alone. It was a delirium too sudden for her fragile psyche and constitution to absorb. She offered the fruit to Adam, who also ate and was likewise transformed into a Kyrios, strong, powerful in his aspect and magnificent in stature. The others present were anxious to partake of the apple, all of them seeking to experience a modicum of the exquisite secret. Even the crickets and mosquitoes wanted to be kyrioses too. Toads and other batrachians battled at day's end. "One nibble is enough for the grand transformation," screeched the parrot, selling for bananas his place at the head of the line. Then came the Great Kyrios (the elephant), furious and, after questioning the culprits, condemned them to extinction. The world came to an end. The curtain fell. The violators of the established order had encountered their destiny.

As Eve had anticipated, the plot served as a perfect lesson for the proud and the arrogant. The chronic malice, the formal disobedience, pride, envy, primeval sins—all punished by the total extinction of the created world and every living thing it held. With neither pain nor mercy. Undeniably, an ingenious solution. At the last rehearsal, Eve finally explained. Everyone approved the script and happily hoped to surprise the Great Kyrios with a grand philosophical tragedy done in his taste and style and not the usual buffoonery. All were in agreement that it was the best play ever produced.

The serpent (the serpent afterwards excused herself, saying accusingly that everything had been planned by Eve and that she had merely followed the script) to avenge herself against Eve and make her hated by the Kyrios, spoiled everything, with pernicious intent. All because of her envy of the earthworm at not having gotten the role of Eve but that of herself. The truth is that she had always hated herself. She had complained to the Kyrios about her form, the absence of sensual curves, even for her, who never envied anyone for anything, as she thought herself extremely attractive, the most beautiful of animals, and detested having to drag herself on the ground. She wanted legs. Centipede legs would go well on her. Hair, mouth, nose, a magnificent vulva down below. She greatly admired the eyes of cats. Oh, if only she had the peacock's tail! Why hadn't she been born, at least, like the earthworm, a roseate color, seductive, fondly febrile, brimming with sex appeal, someone everybody seemed to fall in love with on sight? Self-hatred inflames the soul and destroys the fibers of the heart. The love that takes us to heaven is the twin of the hatred that casts us into the abyss. In the hands of the two, we never know where we are, and care little about the end.

The serpent, in an apparent lapse that was in reality perversity, had dropped the seed. The earthworm, quickly and without being noticed, grabbed it before it touched the ground. The disloyal one approached and offered a real apple for the earthworm to eat, knowing beforehand that she would be unable to grasp, much less bite, such fruit. Besides the formal prohibition by the Great Kyrios: "You may not eat that fruit! For the day you eat of it . . ." Touch it? Not even as a jest. The prohibition was clear, severe, and absolute.

"That ancestor of mine," she said, reflectively, breathing deeply in her chest, "the earthworm"—despite her dramatic genius and the ability to improvise, was dumbstruck. The serpent took advantage of this, insisting, gesticulating, and threatening, "Eat it, you pest, eat it, bite into it, go ahead! You're ruining the play, and the audience is noticing . . .! Soon they're going to start booing us! You worthless thing! Eat it, now! Eat it!" She raised her voice. And the audience, thinking it was part of the act, began applauding and shouting, "Eat! Eat! Eat, little worm! Eat!"

And the booing began. Eve, in agony, seeing the total fiasco —her masterpiece that had given her so much work, so many nights of insomnia and agony, conceived part by part—everything going down the drain. Without reflecting, she rushed to save the play however possible, whispering to the earthworm to feign dizziness and fall, slide, and make a quick exit, disappear. And she herself assumed the role and took a few lascivious bites of the apple. And the transformation was immediate. Eve felt like a true kyria, fiery, lubricious, such as had never been seen on Olympus or the Upper Nile. In addition to powerful and arrogant, giving orders to the Great Kyrios himself and, as if possessed, allowing herself to be dominated by the dream of being a queen, she boldly moved forward on her couch, exposing her rosy breasts, her pudenda with open lips adorned with golden down, inviting him to kiss, to make love, wishing to be his bedmate. The Great Kyrios, perplexed, suspended his breathing, while Eve insisted that He eat the fruit also and feel equal to her. The Kyrios, transfixed, wondered what kind of idiocy could this be, uncertain whether he was seeing a drama or a display of concupiscence and arrogance. Eve, without pausing the dramatic thread, closed her eyes, threw her arms toward the sky, and called out hysterically, unable to accept the rejection nor wishing to be a kyria alone. She needed a companion equal to herself and insisted that Adam eat the apple. More flustered than anyone, he devoured the fruit unaware of what he was doing. And immediately feeling like a powerful kyrios, he advanced toward the Great Kyrios and demanded He yield his throne and bow down before him. "Behold your new Lords, the new kyrioses of the universe!" "Come, get up!" And Adam moved to take the throne. Eve had remained behind him, less daring.

It was still a magnificent piece of staging, a shocking improvisation to provoke the fury of the Great Kyrios and thereby destroy the world He had created, to return everything to the dust of nothingness. The work of the elephant, which she had rehearsed and explained a thousand times, the pose, the imposing voice, the majesty with which he was to shout, "Let the world be undone!" The elephant, however, behind the curtain, confused by the improvised changes and maneuvers and awaiting the cue from Eve to enter and launch the terrible cry, began running back and forth, lifting his trunk, shaking his tail, shooting off his mouth and bellowing like a lunatic. The other actors yelled at him: "Shut up, you! Stick that trunk up your ass!" Not knowing what he was doing, he penetrated himself with it and blew there inside.

Everything went haywire. Even though the public thus far didn't notice anything. The tragedy on stage was turning into a tragedy in real life, while retaining the appearance of an authentic farce. Eve, experiencing her role. She and Adam, experiencing the metamorphosis through which they had never passed, ably presented, the audience in suspense, electrified by the magic power of the staging.

The serpent, upon seeing the failure of her plan, pretends to faint and falls shivering. As if breathing, she shouts hoarsely to the audience, urging everyone to eat the apples before they're annihilated. Not by the Great Kyrios, but by Adam and Eve, two monsters who judged themselves superior to the Great Kyrios himself, telling Him to worship them. Because if they too ate of the apple, they would become their rivals, be wise and powerful like them, capable of creating for themselves other worlds, other lands, other heavens, where they would live in bliss, powerful kyrioses of the world.

Those present started to move forward as a single body, no

one wanting to die, each of them desiring to be immortal; the apple held the secret. They rushed onto the stage. Insane bedlam. Cain and Abel, their siblings and cousins. Disobedience was implanted on Earth. Greed, the veiled desire to supplant the Creator.

The Almighty, seeing this, couldn't control himself any longer and became furious. He interrogates Eve, interrogates Adam, interrogates the serpent, who is still on the ground, playing dead, murmuring things against the kings of creation. As incredible as it seemed, the Great Kyrios accepts the liar's explanation even as he condemns her all the same. In any case, He is totally disappointed and regrets having created the world. Irritated to the extreme, He rose and shouted to the four winds: "Let man and every beast that moves on the face of the Earth be no more!"

The elephant finally appears and yells, "Hey, that's my line!" And repeats after Him: "Let man and every beast that moves on the face of the Earth be no more!"

It was the last thing that was heard. In an instant, everything turned to ashes. A desert of ashes, endless sterility under the sky. And the Great Kyrios vanished for good. Where to? Where did the immortal Great Kyrios, ruler of Heaven, the Earth and the infernal realms, go?

Only the earthworm, so embarrassed she had dug into the ground, remained there, quivering in terror, hearing and seeing everything but unseen by all. Trembling, confused. All life on Earth destroyed. Man, animals, fishes, stars, and plants. All blown to dust. She alone had escaped alive. Happy and unhappy at the same time, finding herself alone in such a large and deserted world. She feared her fate. Suddenly, an inspiration: the seed! The seed is there, the seed her enemy had dropped when she handed over the apple. The microscopic seed of the knowledge of good, evil, and reason. The seed of life. It was her role in the tragedy. Before the serpent ruined everything. Before Eve replaced her, and she, ashamed, burrowed into the soil. She decided to launch the seed. Ah, why not? Eve had said it was a microcosm. Without understanding fully what she was doing, the threw the seed. And behold, as in a dream, everything reappeared. Eve, Adam, the animals, the plants, everything moving, wandering about, everything as it was and had always been. Was she dreaming before or dreaming now? What was shadow? What was image? Where was real life? Man, woman, birds in the sky and fishes in the water. And above all, the fatal tree in the center of paradise. Lovely, seductive. Full of beautiful apples. Eve and Adam rushed toward it, devoured as much as they wanted. And after them, the birds, the animals, both tame and wild, even crickets and fireflies, all of them biting into the apple. And nothing happened. No one thought any further about the terrible fable. But the Great Kyrios . . . He had disappeared without explanation. To where? To where?

 The world became the one we know even today, sometimes sad, sometimes confusing, sometimes strangely happy. With that perpetual longing for the days of paradise. Everything as if it were a drama, a comedy, a bad dream, and the final tragedy, a play in vivid colors, staged by Eve with the best of intentions. It wasn't possible that the Creator took offense at such an innocent play. What damnable evil could there be in the bite of an apple? A desert world had replaced paradise. Was it believable what had happened? Could the earthworm actually be dreaming?

Chapter Twenty

Eve lived many years and had countless children and grandchildren and great-grandchildren and great-great-grandchildren. Just in her last spring, she had five dozen great-great-great-grandchildren, something inconceivable for any woman then or now. At the end of her life, when she was asked how it had happened, how the great tragedy had been, she replied: "It was all my doing. A diversion to enliven the nights in paradise." And if they insisted on knowing what had become of the Great Kyrios, Lord of the world, she would turn red, prettier than ever, even if more unhappy, close her eyes, and after a pause, add in a melancholy tone, "All my doing. All a diversion to enliven the nights in paradise."

The fact is that no one knew of the existence or the whereabouts of the Great Kyrios. Deep down, everyone blamed Eve for the bad-taste play. But she wasn't at fault. It was the envious serpent, dissatisfied with her role. She wanted to act alongside Adam and earn kudos from the Creator. Confessed our first grandmother that at the last instant, when the serpent insisted she eat the apple, and repeated, "Eat it, you worthless thing, eat it," and she decided to assume the role herself, the serpent whispered that none of it was more than the trick of an envious being, evident in the eyes, the voice, and the entire body. Despite this, Eve paid no attention and ordered her to leave the stage at once, immediately, to simulate fainting and disappear into the ground.

The serpent, who had heard everything, became a mortal

enemy forever. Of Eve and especially of the earthworm. She reinforced her envy and resentment over not having kept the seed and losing the great opportunity to recreate the world. She had sworn the annihilation of the earthworm and the persecution of Eve, the posterity of one, the posterity of the other. Because of this, till the end of time, her descendants would not feel safe anywhere, forced to live underground. where they would build their humble dens, living out their wretched lives, unknown to the world, scorned by people.

Chapter Twenty-One

This is common knowledge, something talked about nowadays. However, the story of the earthworms and their influence in history was only beginning. Here, she sighed, stirred a little, elegantly raised one leg, tossed her head back like someone shaking her curls, but she shook loose an idea, perhaps intriguing and rather silly, then smiled like a star at the shark, who was stunned by the final episode of the tragedy, and continued:

Look (she said), even though no history book mentions it, the fight between Cain and Abel was caused by earthworms. A quarrel based on envy among them, before it turned into a tragedy involving the two.

Abel raised the most beautiful earthworms. Cultured, healthy, with a doll's body, graceful and modest, really enchanting. Much in the style and taste of the time. Tempting and divine. Cain's, on the other hand, were sad, stunted, rickety roundworms. The primogeniture of Abel was resented by Cain, who lacked his tact, the smooth and elegant words, the politeness, the passionate glow in the eyes, the romantic gallantry, fruit baskets, bouquets of flowers. Naturally, there arose between them an ongoing dispute and serious quarrels. Not wishing to openly blame their father, they placed the fault on their female cousins, calling them butt-ins, showoffs, vain, arrogant, full of themselves. Given their habit of swinging their hips like models on parade. Attracting attention, provoking whistles. This irritated the cousins even more. They hurled stones at them from the upper windows accompanied by taunts. Abel's earthworms threw the stones back and, for good measure, pulled them from the windows and applied a thrashing in the street. A hullabaloo followed, and the keepers of public order were called. Cain and Abel were questioned, fined as much as the law allowed, and escorted home. Good-humored Abel laughed it off; Cain, irritable as ever, rapped him on the head as usual.

Tempers were not easily calmed. Seeing his brother upset and depressed, Abel, in good physical condition, attempted to smooth over relations. He decided to repeat a family joke, not realizing the implicit injury. "Hey, brother, they took after us! Remember when we used to bet candy over who could piss further and the whole family always bet on me? And you got mad and threw the candy in my face?!"

Evacita, the youngest sister, was too little at the time to recall the incident. Now, she served as companion to them both, sleeping with one, then the other, though she didn't conceal her preference for the younger brother. So, Evani, the older sister, would take her place. With her, Cain sired many children since her early years, and she had decided to abandon him in favor of the middle brother, Abelard, the tallest and most muscular of the three.

His name really was Adelard, which meant son of Adam, just as Adel meant Little Adam. But they had difficulty pronouncing the *d*, for which they substituted *b*, resulting in the current form.

Evacita was so taken with the anecdote that she swallowed a tooth, smiling. The brothers fell to violent slaps and punches. Without, however, serious consequences because Evacita, in exchange for her kisses and promises, could even make the sun stand still, much less soothe the squabbles of her husbands. Until the day of the legendary wager of the bonfire.

In general, games constituted the major diversion for the

family at the end of the day. Everyone took part, they established rules, rooted noisily for their candidates, taunted the others. The worst of all, Adam, goaded his sons to ever more violent jests. Which at first had been bets for sweets, fruits, animals, their own children, sometimes; others', affectionate for a night, a year, or a lifetime. They bet their wives and husbands, and when they no longer had them, the wives and husbands of others. The use of someone else's wife or husband was acquired through concessions, obligations, interest on this, that, and the other. Even Eve often found herself the object of trades made by her husband, forced to sleep with her sons.

Physical beauty weighed heavily, while personality and affection were worth gold. Personal attractions varied greatly with the individual and might be of any order or nature. Thus, marriages burgeoned, unexpectedly, like an agreeable and free union, without the least intention or obligation of permanence. Women, in general, behaved like flowers in the meadow. And men, like bees. In exchange for kisses and caresses, the flowers delivered honey. How sweet was that childhood in paradise! A poet would later sing:

> Oh, how I yearn for
> The dawn of paradise
> Now gone, lost to me
> And the years bring no more.

> What love, what dreams, what flowers
> On those carefree days
> In the shade of apple trees
> And orange groves.

The winner would get to spend an entire month with Evacita. A prize and then some in those days. They had to use products of their labor. Cain, a resolute economist, based on sound Republican principles, dried beans, wheat, rice, and corn, taking advantage of being free of the rotting, mosquito-infested fruits in his backyard. In direct opposition to the liberal current, which didn't allow touching the mosquitos, excellent fuel for the bonfires at day's end. Abel, a diplomat, mystic, and practical philosopher at the same time, chose the three fattest and wooliest sheep from the flock.

Adam opened the ceremonies, offering a moving prayer to the Great Kyrios, who was watching everything from the clouds with one hand on his chin and a sidewise look, after which He himself launched a torch onto the bonfires.

Cain couldn't stand it when the smoke spread and the flames crackled around Abel's sheep. His hatred for his brother knew no limit when he learned the prize had secretly been agreed upon in advance between the two and not openly chosen by the rooters, as stipulated by the established rules. When questioned, like a man, Abel did not deny it. Cain was furious and brought a cudgel down on his brother's skull, splitting it in the middle.

A cold death mask stamped itself on Abel's face. It was the first time anyone had appeared like that, with the mask of sleep, in the brightness of day, without breathing, without responding, without reacting. The work of demons, it was said, though they had never seen one. Calling to him, shouting out his name, shaking him, a kick in the butt, nothing did any good. Abel had left life behind.

Cain fled in panic. The shadow ran after him, hiding him here, there, passing between his legs, waiting for him up ahead and making faces like a phantasm. He started to tremble, to fear everything he saw around him. Certain that someone was arming himself to kill him at any moment. He wet his pants. He dug a hole in the sand and hid his face. Well away from the flames that continued over the fat of the sheep. The Creator came to see the madness up close. He asked: "Cain, where is your brother Abel?" Without taking his face from the sand, he replied: "Am I my brother's keeper?" A rude answer, one not to give to one's elder, much less to the constituted authorities. The Creator, who from the beginning demonstrated his opposition to the death penalty, instead of dispatching the miscreant, subjected him to a few light chastisements. Cain, clever and crafty, began to whine and weep. The Creator, instead of remaining firm, as is required of a Judge, stalled and promised: "Whosoever kills Cain, upon him will fall a vengeance seven times greater." And, as if this were not enough, "Jehovah placed on Cain a mark so that none who might encounter him would put him to death." It was the deal of immunity, a reward. Not too bad for someone who until a short time before pissed himself and ran from his own shadow.

It shows that, from its inception, justice was unjust. On the other hand, one must admire the Creator's perspicacity and extraordinary foresight in adopting our system of partial and selective justice. According to the prevailing vogue and the appearance of the individuals. *"La raison du plus fort est toujours la meilleure"* ["The reason of the strongest is always the best"] as La Fontaine would say.

One questions, here, the Creator's sense of justice, Justice uncreated, in keeping with his most expert biographers and historians. If death came as punishment for disobedience, and if Adam and Eve were the ones who provoked it, why did the first punishment strike precisely the creature of greatest integrity, who neither lied nor deceived, the victim of envy, precisely for having offered a purer and more pleasing sacrifice to the Creator? If you disagree, let's examine the facts. Abel, who was just, loses his life immediately. His parents, who supposedly brought the misfortune into the world and death for everyone, were punished, yes, but capital punishment was postponed. The Creator, like a dotty uncle, still thought to weave for them "tunics of skin."

He had reached his moment of maximum weakness. Completely dispirited, he allowed violence, rebellion, arrogance, the new fruits of the Earth to grow, which would not exist had he eliminated Cain.

While the evildoer fled, the spectacle of death took root there. Abel, his mouth open and staring at the sky. The parents cried, the brothers and sisters wept, the young children understood nothing at all, the women were inconsolable, tore their garments and slashed their breast, the men covered themselves with ashes. The animals shook their heads, whispering to one another, "You see? . . . we kill to live; they kill for revenge." Angels who visited the Earth, and others tasked with some mission to men, stared wide-eyed, stunned, transfixed. They all remembered the words of the Great Kyrios. In saying, "Let us make man in our image and semblance," did He have in mind the perverse nature of Cain?

Chapter Twenty-Two

Evacita cried over the death of her brother and lover with supreme mourning, unceasingly for nine moons and ninety suns. During which time Cain persisted in seeking her every night, spying on her in the thickets, following her to the river. But she never gave in until the period of mourning was over.

He had completely changed his life, treating the earthworms with the same delicacy as had his brother. They became princesses again, loved, kissed, caressed. Day and night, love and more love. Patriarchs and kings followed his example, from Methuselah to Noah, Noah to Solomon.

"After the flood, they called them 'bait,' but they hated the nickname, always preferring 'earthworm,' an affectionate name that recalled paradise. I like clarifying this," said the earthworm, "so people can recognize our nobility of blood, of origin, in our form, our bearing, our line of conduct."

Clyto the shark here nodded his head in confirmation, as he gazed at her with simulated passion. Which was not lost on the earthworm, who saw in it the stupidity of the male who can't control his impatience. No one fools those gurus of the soul, used to detecting even the slightest symptoms of emotion.

They were the first to enter the ark, enveloped by the affection of Noah and his family. There, they multiplied rapidly. A fortuitous incident however, came to seal their fate. The fishes in the waters reproduced in astonishing numbers. Food soon became in short supply, and they began devouring each other.

One fish would devour another fish so voraciously that it in turn was devoured by the very fish it had just swallowed. The forebears of the Amazon piranha were recognized, then, for feeding better inside the stomach than outside. In fact, they wandered in gangs, offering themselves as a meal. Some, more imaginative than the rest, would hang out on corners with a sign in their lapel that, in their dialect, read "Anyone for piranha today?" They even invented a ditty that became very popular in the waters of the river-ocean:

> Piranha, piranha
> Let's all piranhate
> When the piranhas are biting
> Don't get there late.

Naturally, such prostitution was illegal and was reported to Public Order and the Department of Pisciculture. The piranhas defended themselves with artifice, saying that the fishes' hunger had become so severe that any measure, however short-lived, was preferable to starving. Just the opposite, they died satisfied, singing:

> How sweet to die in the sea
> In the waves of the river-ocean . . .

Despite this, their argument would have failed if not for the support of their colleagues, experienced in the art and with much influence in Congress. After a great deal of debate, they finally approved the piranhas' advertising, but forced them to append to the ad the danger to which the partakers of that meal were exposed. Nevertheless, they invented another jingle:

> I die piranhating
> I know quite well
> That if you don't piranhate
> You die anyway . . .

With the full backing of the Libertarian Society, which puts the rights of the citizenry about all else. (Without asking permission this time, the shark suddenly interjected: "My grandfather used to tell me about that period, which is recorded in the annals of our history as the time of the great hunger of the flood. Which some books refer to as having lasted forty suns, when in fact it was forty moons. There are some historians who speak of an uncertain count, since the sun had disappeared totally and the moon, now and then.

"At first, everything went smoothly, as usually happens. With more meat than we could eat. Live meat, raw meat, animal and human meat. So many plants, and everything that was good, floating on the water. Sharks experienced the best days of their lives. Some of our prophets called it the time of fattened cows. Scientists say it was in this phase that we began to grow our several rows of teeth. Eminent marine biologists disagree, arguing that the various layers came from our altruistic desire that the victim not suffer for long. That period was followed by the time of lean cows, which was the great famine of the flood. Unfortunate for the vast majority of fishes but, luckily for us, we suffered no shortfall in our diet. For us, in fact, there never was a thing of lean cows. The so-called phase of lean cows was succeeded by a period of even fatter ones. Because, by swallowing a single fish, medium-sized or large, we were in fact swallowing two or three, one inside the other, in an economy of teeth, jaws, and saliva.")

At this point, Monice looked at him with an irritated expression so venomous that it left him speechless. He lowered his gaze, made an awkward bow, and fell silent. She marveled at the world of difference that goes from earthworm to human, and from man to a beast like that. She understood what blood was, bile, the shark psyche that came to him from the cradle. And her expression revealed a degree of contentment, a mix of pardon and fondness for the monster, to whom she unconsciously felt attracted. There are such people, fatally drawn to someone without knowing why.

The rains had stopped. That was when a very alert and flirtatious earthworm, improvised on the spot the future model of the runway. Lovely in her feminine outfit, swaying seductively, strolling alone on deck, she slipped and fell into the water. The fishes were quickly upon her, in the greatest feeding frenzy in history. Noah and his descendants witnessed the scene, horrified. From that day till now, the fishes of the entire world lose control at the sight of a worm. The phenomenon has become part of their genes. In some cases, it seemed that the more the disparity in size between the two, the crazier they become. (At this moment the shark smiled mischievously, softened his throat in a happy distraction, heaved his chest, but didn't interrupt, except for his watery eyes that gave him that aspect of a hired gun, in the time-honored tradition of baroque sharks.)

The earthworm's destiny as bait was sealed. It should be understood that being devoured is not as bad as it appears. It is not rare for worms to survive the fishes that swallow them whole, returning to land intact. Besides which, any part of an earthworm's body can function as the whole and slowly regenerate itself until reaching its original size. A privilege no other animal on earth enjoys, except maybe the two-headed Caecilian, the cunning descendant of a past enemy.

We flourished in Egypt, Abyssinia, in the oases of vast Arabia. The Queen of Sheba was the first to elevate us to the category of princesses, each with her own major art form, her own practices, her personal enchantment in the conquest of loves, dismissing the idea of husbands, which implies possession, alien by nature to the "genus earthworm," for those lovers were kings and princes, generals, ambassadors, notable governors of provinces from beyond the tomb. They played a role in the conquest of Solomon, a macho king passionate like few others about his showy earthworms. When she went to visit him, she took with her three hundred thousand earthworms, the prettiest and most glamorous in her realm. Solomon quickly crossed them with Jewish earthworms to produce the most desirable species on Earth. A delightful combination of beauty, sensuality, affection, craftiness, and astuteness unknown before. The passion for earthworms became, with the great king, fashionable in the entire country. A voluptuousness that devoured the chest, for the more of them they ate, the more vitality surged, and desire grew. Which lured him away from the moderation and virtue that had brought him to the attention of the Great Kyrios and made him famous through the ages. To such an extent that the prophet Nathan and the people started to fear punishment from the heavens. The austere king ate earthworms in revelries, as a joke. In a single day, the quota common to mortals for a lifetime. A more avid wormeater had never walked the earth. Even though the competition had increased in our times, not to mention his father, David, who passed on to him the insatiable gene. Especially in the category of rulers of territory and peoples. Some were destined not to obtain the presidency because they ate too much. Others because they ate too little. One, a different one, got there through a collusion of the fates and the elements, and no lesser daring. And still others, despite the gift of gab, never realized the dream of making it to the great whitewashed dwelling. Thanks to the Great Kyrios of us all. Such a race of rulers would decimate, once and for all, the "genus earthworm" from the face of the planet.

Solomon consumed a hundred for breakfast, two hundred at lunch, three hundred for dinner, four hundred before sleeping, two hundred when he woke up. He had the habit of spending entire nights playing with hybrid worms from the kingdom, or from Arabia or the neighboring Abyssinia. Uninhibited, solitary, missing his days with the Queen of Sheba, his mind contrite and turned toward Him who had vouchsafed him wisdom, at the end of his life, turning to face the setting sun, he exclaimed his proverbial "*Minhoca minhocarum et omnia minhoca sunt!*" ["Earthworms of the earthworms and all is earthworms!"] A tremendous cry of pain and nostalgia from the great and wise Solomon! The love that burned in his chest was so strong that he insisted on being buried with all of them alive, despite the vehement protests of the prophet Nathan and his colleague prophets and scribes.

In that period, the population of earthworms was six hundred thousand, not counting those faithful to the queen, to whom they vowed to return one day. The result amazed the world from one end to the other. When the tomb of the great king was opened, behold the miracle—the body intact, the skin cool and soft as if just coming from a bath and sleeping a deep slumber. And all of them, determined fighters, combatted the grave-worms like an army relentless in a battle of extermination, not allowing even one to escape, dead or alive, however fearless or cunning. They gave their lives so he, whose love surpassed all, might have the desired immortality. Their cadavers, fresh and soft, like a wreath of roses around his body, from which emanated perfume and seemed to smile in gentle sleep. "Behold," said the learned men studying the tomb, "the six hundred thousand of the king's most faithful!" His lips seemed to be singing a new Song of Songs. Thus, the glory of the great Solomon, after death, grew more than in life.

According to legend, even today the great king continues intact in some part of the Holy Land, by a wreath of his perfumed earthworms. His secret desire, according to the legend, was to be buried with them.

The prophets of the realm, however, were unmoved by the rumors regarding this, given the process of mummification, as they knew well, to be commonplace in Egypt and in the regions of the Upper Nile. And, seeing that they had ironically nicknamed him "king of the earthworms," they now went on to refer to him by other, more insolent titles like "glorious worm man of the Most High." Which sounded like blasphemy and was born from a legitimate rivalry. A goodly number of prophets remained unsure whether they should address him as an equal or a simple mountebank. By telling the Great Kyrios that they condemned the king's manias and derelictions of duty. A bare-faced lie. In order not to have to rain the heavens down on their heads, the Great Kyrios covered his ears every time their lips moved.

They maintained his harem of earthworms, some camouflaged and hidden, others cynical, open to the light of day following the practice of the king and his father David. Still others, captious, conceded to their lovers the profession of divination, treating them as prophetesses and sybils who, often, were only ordinary witches, or advanced technicians. Some, less prophetess but adept in the game of amulets, very pretty, were excellent companions in visions and service. The women were alerted about which days and which nights the Great Kyrios would appear behind the bramble bush, as He had with Moses. The Great Kyrios preferred brambles far from home. And his favorite hour was from nine at night until three in the morning. Let no one dare approach. The place where they trod was holy and reserved for prophets.

In any case, before sleeping, there the Most High was, calling them again, behind the burning brambles. His voice couldn't be clearer. "Prophet, make haste! Take an urgent message to that rebellious people!" Women should pay attention, for they too should hear. They hear nothing, though they aspire to hear. Still, who were they to resist the voice of the Most High? In dreams, they prophesied in ecstasy, speaking of unsullied virgins, sublime bodies, hot-blooded widows. Their song of songs would make Solomon envious. They were ready to vie with the great king for a place in the Bible. And they promised women they would share with them their name and their glory. And mention them always at their side. Resigned and dreamers, the women agreed. It has always been the way of women to believe the lies of their husbands.

Until, one day, a woman grew impatient and tried to confront the Most High. Face to face. The disrespect on the part of the Great Kyrios. His impertinence in interfering in her life. What urgent message was it that kept her husband by the burning bush all night? Three whole years, without him coming for her, whether in bed, by the river, under the fig tree, or during the wheat harvest like the husbands of her neighbors, despite the universal enticements and others, improvised. Except for the honeymoon, goodbye love, goodbye affection, goodbye nighttime embraces.

Following him cautiously, she hid at a distance. She saw how he moved, looking to all sides. But what was that? There was no thicket there, much less a bush. It was the house of a prophet friend of his and his prophetess wife, the most gifted of all in those days. With her Philistine blood and the magic from Abyssinia. Perhaps, who knows, they were going to implore the Great Kyrios to send a little rain, as the drought had already lasted three months.

She boldly advanced and peeked through the window. The Great Kyrios was there nude, in bed, embracing her husband! She was dumfounded by such a marvel and the unsurpassed daring. The Great Kyrios had assumed completely the form of the prophetess. Long dark tresses, eyes wide and lusty like those of Delilah. Her breasts, like roses opening to the dew, slipping through the impatient lips of her transfigured husband.

She had never seen him like that, not even at their first encounter in the thicket, or on the eve of their wedding. Now withdrawing, now allowing herself to be bitten. Tongues passing from each other's mouths, in the greatest traffic of tongues in that part of the planet. A bite here, a bite there, putting everything in the mouth. That was how Philistine women stole husbands. But, where was her husband, the young prophet with burning visions who had left her alone in the splendor of her nakedness, offering to kiss her beautiful cluster of grapes?

The cudgel she was carrying put an end to the celestial visions, leaving burning reminders on back and buttocks. What is certain is, from that day, the Great Kyrios, repentant of what happened, would never again appear to any prophetess in that part of the world. And all the beds in Israel resumed functioning normally with their prophets back. Squeaking hot and perfumed late into the night. Final chapter of the prophecies.

Chapter Twenty-Three

It is known that Aristotle would begin his Anatomy classes with the vivisection of earthworms. To the Sociology classes he would take four: Father earthworm, mother earthworm, earthworm son, along with the earthworm neighbor. And he would say solemnly, "Notice that the earthworm will leave his father and mother and join his fellow earthworm. (In ancient Greek, the noun earthworms had two genders, while in modern languages it kept only one." [Explanation of Monice.]) "And both shall be as one flesh." And he would show the action, the interaction, life alone and in a family, beginning, begun, and finished. Tragically, at times, because with the intention of heightening the drama in a scientific manner, he ordered the lovers to practice amorous peripetias, such as leaping together from a waterfall. Goethe's *Werther* must have been inspired by this. It's no surprise that his classes were always packed, with young people jumping from windows to take part in the suicide.

Sitting next to Alexander, they attended the classes of rhetoric and poetics, music and dance. From which emerged the origins of the minuet and the quadrille. The tango itself was a spontaneous invention of Alexander, a handsome, elegant young man and a peerless dancer both before and after he became famous. Slender, with a dark crystal gaze, an air of command even when asleep, energetic and chivalrous at the same time, long legs too slim for his excellent physique. He had spent the night in one of the biggest revelries of that fall, promoted by his classmates. He woke up with a pain in the hindquarters and a stiff neck. Knowing that he had to present a dance number in class and that he had failed to prepare one, he improvised, picking out the worm with whom he had spent the night, the possessor of rare enchantments and a beautiful sense of innovation, except that she herself couldn't move a muscle. A show like none ever seen. The class applauded deliriously. Aristotle promised a new treatise, which he called "Tango Alexandrino." He had just baptized the dance that would later be reborn in Argentina.

Alexander's later deeds were due to a diet restricted to earthworms. He would fill himself from mouth to gut, without touching anything else, on the eve of battle. His courage grew, his military genius expanded, his feats became incredible, the bravery of his soldiers limitless, and all because of the way he cajoled his earthworms, sometimes piling them up to form fortresses that stood up to lances and poisoned arrows.

Alexander took them to Egypt, where the pharaohs elevated them to the category of divinity. Cleopatra celebrated them, using the same unguents as the Queen of Sheba. From whom would learn Lucretia Borgia, Queen Elizabeth (a solitary worm fancier who was allergic to husbands), and the most tragic of them all, Marie Antoinette. The Austrian princesses saved the country, for no other reason than their earthworms, beautiful, blond, truly golden. Who would guess that the famous lines ". . . *Tu, felix Austria, nubes!*" ["Let others wage war, thou, happy Austria, marry!"] owed exclusively to the appeal of the earthworms? Proof of this is the unimpeachable testimony of the Napoleons and the emperors of Brazil.

Queen Isabella imported earthworms from the New World, managing to keep King Ferdinand in love and faithful. But with

Cleopatra we had truly attained glory. First, with the conquest of Caesar and Mark Antony. Afterward, the crown of Egypt, the heights in Rome. Immortality in marble and gold. All those monuments destroyed, forgotten, expunged from memory. Because eating earthworms in public or behind closed doors became a shameful thing. A law that Solomon would have ripped to pieces. Alexander, burned. Caesar, spat on. Nobody any longer wanted to be seen with earthworms. Even if they met in secret, like the prophets of old.

Chapter Twenty-Four

In the Middle Ages, we suffered plagues of every kind and the Black Death, which almost drove us to total extinction. Despite our being the number one tidbit in palaces, the favorite in monasteries, and the preference of popes and cardinals. Obsession with earthworms was the chic thing of the time. One pope, Alexander IX, only recently discovered by revisionist historians, was nicknamed The Mustache for his pirate eyes and goatee. His reign is confirmed by a coin found near Castel Santangelo. A dwarflike nun put the rust-covered object in her pocket, thinking: In Rome every metal is gold. She had no idea she was resuscitating one of the most picturesque popes in history. A relative of the Borgias, he sired a dozen children before being ordained and became the first grandfather pope since Peter. He tried to canonize his earthworm while it was still living. Which raised objections from more than a few, both within the Church and outside it. The protest was widespread, with even rabbis and Buddhist monks writing inflammatory diatribes. Nevertheless, he was obstinately considering evoking infallibility to impose his point of view. The matter, however, exploded unexpectedly one day when, during the *missa solemnis* of the coronation of the kings of Sicily, the concelebrant, a cardinal with whom he had almost come to blows in the sacristy, climbed to the altar and hurled insults, pinching him beneath his papal paraments. The pope, trying at all costs to maintain the dignity and decorum of the moment, directed a sidelong reverence at him after each pinch, as if it were a liturgical bow, moving his lips and calling on saints not in the calendar: "You son of a wanton! I'll smash your face, you son of a bitch!"

The cardinal's insults stemmed from an old rancor on the part of the Borgia grandfather, a legitimate cousin on his mother's side. They had grown up together, slept in the same bedroom, and gone to the same schools. When his father died, he, his mother, and his siblings were forced to live with their rich relatives. The troublemaking Borgia, the owner of everything, wasn't happy with the intrusion into his family. Don't touch anything, "meddler," unless you want a slap or a severe pinch. He grew up, then, like a bastard in an alien household, cursing his fate, timid, and unloved.

It had been that Borgia, "pirate's gaze and goatee," who had stolen the greatest treasure of life. He whispered to him, "Eulalia, your beloved earthworm, is right there! Next to the altar, looking at you! Bless her, bless her, for all the world to see!"

There was no way the pope, or the other cardinals, could silence him. At the moment of introitus, the pope lost control completely and, instead of saying *Introibo ad altare Dei* [Go to the altar of God.], said: *Introibo ad altare Eulaliae . . .!* [I will enter the altar of Eulalia . . .!] To which the cardinal responded: *Ad Eulaliam quae laetificat juventutem meam!* [To Eulalia, who gladdens my youth!]

A horrified murmur spread through the basilica. The pope's mother fainted in her pew. The men grabbed their handkerchiefs, while the women hid their faces in their head scarves. Only the pope's aged father remained calm, like a statue, looking straight ahead, stiff and deaf. The two, realizing what had happened, embarrassed and biting their lips, abruptly corrected themselves, sensing the scandal and ridicule to which they had exposed themselves, and the holy liturgy, beating their chests and violently intoning mea-culpas, contrite and sheepish at the botched ritual.

Too little and too late. The scandal was consummated. The people, who already knew of everything, as the Vatican bulletins had made public Alexander's quarrel with Cardinal Caprino, now witnessed the perfection of the corpus delicti, a beautiful prioress, with green feline eyes, hands raised to Heaven in rapt prayer, enthralling all who saw her. Her air of a saint, in her form and her entirety, kept the heart ablaze with lust.

She was the cardinal's former lover since boyhood. Neither becoming a bishop nor donning the robe of cardinal extinguished the old ardor. The cardinal wanted her back at any cost, even life itself. He promised himself that he would poison the pope with the sacramental bread and wine. He already had a letter signed by the vintner and sealed by the baker. If one failed, the other wouldn't. By his calculations, the pope should collapse on the steps exactly when he was intoning the *Ite* in a choked and trembling voice ... *Vita est!*

Cardinal Caprino's revenge didn't end there. In order not to waver from his intent, through weakness or intervention of Grace (which, from one moment to the next could ruin everything), he, who had never been a poet, wrote down on paper some rancid lines that even the demon charged with tempting him shrank from reading:

> 'Tis necessary to put an end to Borgia
> Using the bread and wine of the Mass
> I shall see him convulsing
> In parament and all.

Cardinal Anulfo Caprino would never perpetrate the crime. Denounced by the baker but not by the vintner, whose harvest he had guaranteed for three years, he was expelled from the Church and solemnly excommunicated. He would die insane in an alleyway, ragged and filthy at the side of his lover, singing and clutching an empty bottle against his naked chest.

> Eulalia, my dearest
> The flower of Andalusia
> It was you who taught me
> The love I never knew.

This, however, would only happen years and years later. Now, he couldn't bear to see her. Seeing her was enough to destroy nerves exhausted by a futile passion. Cardinal Caprino, whom many called simply "Cabreal," sunken brow, dark hair cut very short, deep-set eyes of a fox, thin arms and legs of a seriema tree, whose appearance gave him the false image of an ascetic, died of love from the sight of the prioress and hating to see her so close. He envisioned the stifled kisses, the fevered embraces, the sempiternal vows of love that in dreams they exchanged countless times. Even before puberty erupted in them both, before he grew the dark mustache and she the blond carpet, pubescent and sparse. Swearing that she hated Borgia and would never yield to his advances and gallantries. She couldn't even tolerate his pimply face, his fetid breath. She swore she would never let him touch her body. Swore. Swore as she kissed him. Her virgin heart was still hers, hers alone, all hers, eternally hers. And no one else's in the world. "Heaven, hell, death—nothing, angel or demon, would take her from his arms." These were eternal vows, between eternal and breathless kisses.

There were phases when the "cabreal" showed signs of passion for the priesthood. He based his sermons on the types of spirituality most in fashion and always cited the great spiritual celebrities of the period. He wrapped himself in that air of asceticism that clung to his body even after the fever subsided and lust returned. Young men and women, after confessions, took him as spiritual guide. They allowed themselves to be hugged and sat in his lap to better imbibe his sacred counsel.

Borgia would stun the entire country upon becoming a cardinal as a formality before the papacy. Also, his advances diminished since a new affair with his first cousin, Anestella, who had arrived from Sicily. Anestella, of Austrian blood, tall and slender, with generous breasts that were the center of attention, sung by poets as roses of paradise, in contrast to Eulalia's, which severe critics attributed to the beasts of the Apocalypse. Tourmaline eyes. A perfect doll from eyelashes to ankles. A languid walk and affectionate, which would lead to six offspring before she wasted away, discontent, in a convent. While he, because of his new office, had to abandon her with the children, went off to Eulalia's bed. More precisely, when she threw herself into his arms upon seeing him for the first time with the cross on his chest, the soft crimson and the white ermine. And not long afterwards, the pontifical crown.

What went on between the two is not recorded. Not even in the few pages of the diary they left behind. She, to disguise her meetings with Borgia, had accepted the position of prioress, and abandoned him without ever giving him an excuse or reason. He, blinded by love and the will not to admit defeat, had accepted from his enemy the pope a rich bishopric and the cardinal's hat, something he had never thought about in his wildest dreams. At least he could now go see her whenever he wished.

Now, in the Mass, they looked at each other out of the corners of their eyes, turned their noses up, and gave fierce grunts whenever they accidentally made eye contact. Distant, barbed, sporadic. At the discreet request of the king, the prioress withdrew during the ceremony. As she was crossing the portal of the church, the pope unexpectedly invoked her in the memento for the saints, causing an even greater scandal than the first: "St. Eulalia! . . . *ora pro nobis* . . ." In prayers, flying to the heavens, the cardinal made him descend to Earth, by way of a tremendous pinch. "Stop that," "Cuckold," "Faggot," "Son of a whore!" "I'll bust your face right now! I swear it!" The concelebrants were already accustomed to such alexandrine invective.

That same night, an urgent request arrived. Eulalia was to appear in the pontiff's chambers. For a most serious consultation, "a matter of the Faith, his Holiness couldn't sleep, or leave it for another day." And there went Eulalia in the middle of the night, accompanied by the sisters in a candlelight procession, with the Swiss guard in front, to the door of the private library. Alexander had received her there. The doors closed, and the sisters returned to their cells, heads lowered, candles extinguished, the psalms of David falling from their lips, insipid and without meaning.

Chapter Twenty-Five

Before he died, however, Cardinal Caprino had filled Spanish newspaper pages with picaresque and strange things. He started hearing celestial voices. He distinctly heard the Archangel Gabriel ordering him to take off his clothes, light a candle in broad daylight, and go looking for Eulalia, lost in some alleyway. And when he thought he had found her, he announced: "Hail Eulalia, full of grace!" And when the announced one ran in fright, saying she wasn't Eulalia, he would run after her, trying to convince her she was.

He ended up in jail several times, but the voice of Gabriel persisted. Despite everything, he became an amiable crazy and would always find someone who accepted the message. Still, after the tender mistake, he would come to his senses and begin to beat the impostor who was trying to pass as his beloved. Not infrequently, both would be hauled off to jail.

Chapter Twenty-Six

Now, the drunks of the region, and even people who didn't drink, found in all of this a priceless plot for a novel and, whether as a joke or from malice, began adopting the system of angelical greeting. The Third Order of the Topers of Alkançakevir was established. There are people even today who protest against this historical scandal, with the most conservative bastions of the good name of Spain flinging into the sea the archives and burning any reference to the fact, however slight. Nevertheless, they were helpless to destroy the legend rooted deep in the heart of the people.

Alkançakevir . . . "garden of Spain / that the sunset kisses first," as a Baroque poet standing on the seashore once sang, had become a peaceful place after being one of the bravest bulwarks in the resistance to Islam. The setting for numerous memorable battles, "attacked in the flanks / with iron, fire and bullet / without ever seeing the vile Moor gain advantage." Land of the "heroic *pantorras*" and the "gallant fins," illustrious warriors in the expulsion of the Muslims.

None of them, however, greater than Sergeant Felício, who practically lived in a jail cell, but who as a young man had become immortal and the idol of all for having singlehandedly defended the largest fort in the city against three hundred invading Moors. How he had done it is known by few, and even fewer spoke of it in order not to denigrate the legendary feat and thereby sully the bravery of the Sergeant. For decades, he had personified the courage, the honor, the valor of the Spanish soldier.

Felício quickly saw in the craziness of "Cabreal" a means of restoring himself and reliving his days. He burned his clothing, lit a candle, and placed himself at the head of the movement, lending it his name and erstwhile charisma. His name, however, had dimmed and the legend was so moribund that only a handful of people knew of him and even fewer greeted him in the streets.

It was with bitterness that he remembered everything. At the age of fifteen, he had had Spain at his feet. He was on everyone's lips. There had never been a greater hero, a greater feat had never been seen. The pride of a nation. Decorated, carried triumphantly through the streets in an open carriage. Galloons on his shoulders, medals on his chest. The ceremonial golden rapier on his belt. In public parades, everyone wanted to see him up close, to touch him, hug him, young women insisting on kissing him on the mouth. They offered themselves with conduct, words, winks. Parents practically handed over their daughters. His entrance into mansions, palaces, or simple homes of the people had become an acquired right. An honor that made the neighbors envious and gave enemies something to talk about. He would arrive unexpectedly and sit down without being invited. And it was in this way that he came to manhood, swimming in emoluments, as if the attraction that he aroused in women, the envy and admiration in men, would never end.

His appetite, which knew no limits, drove him to seek in other cities what was lacking in his own. And, since cities in Spain were not numerous and offered few women to adore him on sight, he crossed the Pyrenees, wandered about Italy in search of hot-blooded young women and accepted invitations that came to him from Calabria and Sicily. Ten years went by like this in a paradise that no man on Earth had dreamed of or possessed. Unable to tolerate seeing his prestige evaporate and old loves flee, he began taking by force that which he was no longer offered. He even raped, in broad daylight, a girl who had never heard his name, an inconceivable offense. A hero of the country treated like a nobody...

His moments of glory came to mind. He recalled the carriages overflowing with flowers, the presence of the king and queen, the cardinal, the ministers, the band playing military music. The reception in the palace, the *missa pontificalis* in the public square, the chorus of castrati youths. The vows of love from the most beautiful and appetizing women. What came to mind most of all was his moment of great inspiration.

Alone in the command tower, seeing the enemy approaching, the sole survivor in the midst of so many dead comrades, the fortress now empty, without a single musket to defend it, watching his fatherland fall into the hands of infidels. Then, the inspired moment. His moment of glory. He quickly gathered his fallen comrades into a pile, set it ablaze, and found a safe hiding place. There was so much flesh that the blaze would last all night. Some black birds, attracted by the smell, perched and waited nearby for it to cool. On one foot then the other, they cawed, anticipating the feast. When the Moors saw the cadavers smiling at them and the crows feasting, they thought they were seeing demons delighting in a banquet. Feet, do your thing; they ran, and some say they're still running.

All these stories would just be tavern gossip had Pope Alexander IX, the one with the mustache, alarmed by the scandal of the Order and the fame lent to it by Sergeant Felício (promoted to major, they never stopped referring to him as sergeant) not decided to excommunicate him publicly by means of a scathing bull. He had done so arbitrarily, without consulting those in the taverns, infallible in the area of rumors and customs. Which only whetted the public's appetite and resulted in something no one imagined. Because in a few months the adepts of the scandalous Order numbered in the scores in the most remote parts of the province. Imagine, even conservative members of the clergy were abandoning priestly garb without adopting any other, to carry in person the messages of the Archangel Gabriel to the privileged virgins of the village. At the height of the legend, the nuncio apostolico, in those days considered the most likely candidate to the papacy, who had come in person to excommunicate the delinquents, ended up converting and took to the streets with an entire convent, burning candles and endowments to the wind.

This news infuriated Cardinal Caprino, and his Angel Gabriel became so sad that, covering his face with his wings, he cried like a child. From then on, the messages from the celestial troubadour ceased. Also, the Cardinal went back to wearing clothes and, hugging the empty bottle of sherry, closed his eyes and improvised tender and touching serenades. Even today, the Cardinal's fame lives in the streets and his sentimental songs were never forgotten.

> You were my life
> La . . . lia, you left me so soon
> Lalia, Lalia, Lalia,
> You went away and never returned . . .
> Don't forget,
> Beloved Lalia

The enchantment that shone in my eyes
But all the love you had for me
Was so little that the Devil hauled it away . . .

Chapter Twenty-Seven

But fate was closing in. Eulalia finally yielded to the true love of her life. She fled the convent to be with him in a place where no one knew them. They died poor, ragged, begging in the street, as happy as Job.

Shocked by the news, the Pope saw in it the designs of Providence. A moral jolt, a cruel remorse that moved him to tears. Also, it was the first time in history that a pope displayed compunction over a cuckold's pain. He reconsidered his first impulse, to bring Eulalia to Rome. Far from him to separate what Heaven had so clearly united. He ordered a grave to be opened for the pair in the same small corner of the garden where they had first met. Even today, Alkançakivir, the tomb of the Cardinal and Eulalia is covered with flowers. Thousands of bees appear daily, tasked with transforming into honey the sorrow of a passion that had no equal since the days of Abelard and Heloise.

Chapter Twenty-Eight

Monice paused her narration a bit, her throat dry, which gave the shark the opportunity to repeat his chivalrous bow and bring to her lips a few drops of water. Her gesture of gratitude was promising. Luckily, the shark, emotional at having been able to move closer to her again, didn't notice anything. He returned to his earlier position, sensually licking his lips, eager not to miss a syllable or the slightest intonation.

There were places, she continued, where the gluttons of the faith, cynical types taking advantage of people's innocence, created sanctuaries and pedestals, erected countless altars and monuments. Even a gilded temple was dedicated to a certain Queen of the Earthworms of the Orient. It housed images of privileged earthworms and saints still alive, and in her name, pilgrimages were made throughout the world. The truly faithful prayed, obtained miracles, lit candles. Because, it must be stressed, miracles are not something that happens from outside in, but rather from the inside out. Each one is capable of turning desire into a living reality.

We became the preferred saints of the monasteries and convents, the nymphs of nobles and feudal lords. We inspired saints and mystics, theologians, philosophers, professors of sciences sacred and profane, writers and poets, from the unknown to the great. Dante, Petrarch, Torquato Tasso, and the immortal Cervantes were our companions at revelries and orgies. Goethe devoured us on his knees, good Teuton that he was, eyes closed, enraptured in a dream, living in flesh and blood Werther's passion. It was a drama we staged that inspired the loves of Doctor Faust and the annoyances of Mephistopheles. We made Mephistopheles appear, in the form of a male earthworm, dour and grave, mysterious, austere. In exchange for lovemaking, he promised all the world's beauty, health, good fortune, treasures. Goethe was enchanted by that. And he became a kind of Apollo of our time.

As a child Shakespeare would take them to bed, and one day he asked them to stage the tragedy of *Othello*. And afterwards, *Romeo and Juliet*. In the original, actually, Juliet didn't kill herself until the Romeo earthworm plunged a thorn into his chest and died because of her. The fatal mistake always embarrassed us and forced our best actresses to abandon the stage once and for all.

It's necessary to understand that, since that instant of Eve's fatal error, we have experienced the drama of men from the perspective of ourselves. Despite appearances, we feel responsible for everything, the shock we caused you, for displacing you from the state you were in and giving you a world like this.

The Bard of Albion was the only one willing to recognize publicly that the masterpieces of the entire world, especially those involving the history of the empire, were inspired by the love of earthworms, both as symbol and reality, if not for the fatal order of the virgin queen who foresaw the discrediting of the throne and her very name. A caricature of the time depicted Elizabeth devouring an earthworm larger than the Tower of London. English humor—in which *verum et humor* don't always harmonize—sometimes goes from the bizarre to sublime ridicule. The royal camel became famous when it squatted to sip the spillage from a female camel belonging to a commoner. Or something of the sort.

It is worth remembering that without the Anglo-Saxons, the legitimate heirs of the Romans in the prowess of their deeds, just as without the French, heirs of the Greeks in the art of words, ours would be a world of backward and handicapped earthworms.

With the poets, we spent nights amusing ourselves, perhaps more than in the times of Solomon and Alexander. In truth, there is no vestige of this in the pages of History; under pressure from public opinion and thanks to a weakness that prevails among geniuses, all the evidence was destroyed. When asked, they openly denied our presence in their lives, cynically and hatefully. And the memory of the people, subservient and mute, always prefers to acquiesce rather than express itself in a different fashion.

Camões, however, was a genius who came to save the class of poets. He restored honor to them, along with the memory and dignity of bygone times. And it was following a good dish of earthworms that he composed the most beautiful verses in the language, his ninth canto, the orgiastic celebration on the Isle of Love. There, in the Palace of Tethys, the "Governor of Heaven and peoples" willed that we appear as "aquatic damsels," disguised as irresistible naiads, beautiful nymphs. We seduced the brave Portuguese men, just as we had seduced Alexander, Caesar, and even Ulysses, contrary to Homer's falsification. The Florentine cast us into Hell and into paradise, in the images and enigmas of the divine tercets of the Comedy. So, everywhere we lived under the mysticism of symbols, bolstering the treatment that men afford us, ignoring that we are princesses in breeding and origin, not despicable worms that feed on mud. Who today remembers Solomon in the apotheosis of life exclaiming in ecstasy: *"Minhoca minhocarum et omnia minhoca sunt!*"?

The singer da Gama, enraptured, once expressed himself: "Ah, little things of my life, if I found the foot of an earthworm, I would even eat small green earthworms!"

Lovely, lovely, that! When my mother would tell me about it, and even today when I recall it, I suffer anguish in my entrails. A good son of Portugal was he, known as *trinca-fortes*! Another like him was never seen nor ever will be seen in fertile Lusitania!

Anathema to King Sebastian and his court, which awarded him a paltry pension of merely 15,000 réis, tantamount to casting him into poverty. Anathema to the Portuguese of the period, who allowed their greatest hero of all time to be "tossed into a trench, without psalm, without accompaniment, wrapped in a sheet because he had not even a coffin, with other victims of the plague . . .," his bones and ashes forever unrecognizable, a bard greater than the Florentine, than the man from Mantua, than the blind poet from Chios. Singer, unifier of the language, of the culture, of Portuguese glories. Anathema, a thousand times, to those to blame for all this. Even if it's the tradition of great men, from Moses to Mozart, to have no tomb where their name would be remembered and their bones find repose.

Cabral is said to have let himself be misled by a friar, private secretary and friend, a scribe who in secret devoured not only earthworms but also grasshoppers, and who presented the king a platter of wasps. Cabral had packed his flagship with the most beautiful Portuguese earthworms. In Brazil, they were crossed with those from there, producing the models who lend enchantment to the beaches and inspire poets and troubadours.

In that saddest and most catastrophic of times, the Lisbon earthquake took place. On that first of November 1755, the churches were packed with people, along with fifty thousand Portuguese earthworms, the most beautiful, noble and enviable in the realm. Even today, it is not understood why the Great Kyrios treated lovable creatures that way. If it were at least the Day of the Dead. . . . But on All Saints Day! What sarcasm! Perhaps, repenting of having created the world, he wanted to destroy it again, mirroring Samson when he clutched the columns in the temple and shouted: "Let Samson die and the philistines!" No eyewitness heard a shout of any kind, whether inside the walls of the temple or coming from the heavens: "Let the Great Kyrios die and the people of Lisbon!" He didn't die in the least. He was hidden then, and remained hidden. It would be a case of people asking: Would the Great Kyrios love the world so much that he would send such an earthquake? Would he?

Even Voltaire, a genius of good sense, of sarcasm and humor, not that much of poetry, was moved. (Some say that his Henriade is nothing but balky fawning, and who knows if that's why he envied Camões and mistreated Shakespeare.) And he mocked Portugal any time he got the urge. But why, Voltaire, so much acrimony in comparing that misfortune to an *auto-da-fé*? It was the greatest slaughter in history since the days of Pompeii, and the Great Kyrios seems like a Jesuit executioner. A repugnant, cowardly act. Taking advantage of people of good faith inside their churches. How can that be understood, oh heartless Kyrios? Everyone, from the educated to the simple, was revolted and wanted to prosecute the Great Kyrios. Put Him in jail in the middle of the night and throw away the key. Accused of killing fifty thousand Portuguese and fifty thousand earthworms! The local government attorney summoned Him to appear in the court of men. But the Great Kyrios ignored it. The prosecutor shouted in desperation: "Kyrios, oh Kyrios, where are you that you don't respond? In what world, what star are you hiding? Huddling in the sky?" (One hundred years later, other monstrosities would inspire similar questions.) "If you are Father, if you are Good, if you are all they say you are, if after all you are Just, come here and explain yourself to the good people of Portugal, who light a million candles, who pray daily millions of rosaries, attend every day endless Masses, pray novenas, and have built twelve thousand churches in foreign lands, and live with a stomach bulging with sardines, respond to our inquiry, justify yourself to the good Portuguese people!" The prosecutor outdid himself, eloquently demanding with metaphors, images, and threats that the "Governor of Heaven and of peoples" appear there to reveal himself. But He turned a deaf ear and didn't move an inch, take pity, or accuse himself. As if he were saying in his mortal silence: "You imbecilic people, what do you want of me at this time?!" The prosecutor threatened to close the doors of the churches and send the Jesuits to the guillotine. "Bring to me six just ones in the mold of Ignatius, or I'll order the blades to be sharpened!" They found two, or rather, one and a half. The loyal son of Loyola, a righteous Molinist, in addition to his sight, had lost his arms and legs in the earthquake. The judge was quibbling when a loud thunderclap rattled the roof tiles. The courtroom filled with light and turned as golden as a Portuguese Sistine chapel. The Great Kyrios appeared there, by now old and bearded, wearing peasant clothing, wrinkled and showing no sign of ever having been ironed, a poor wretch outwardly, but majestic and dignified in his gaze, surrounded by angels that held him up, as if his legs wouldn't obey him.

His reply stunned the court of Lisbon and the Portuguese

people. Speaking with the voice of thunder, he stated clearly and in good tone for them to go to China! That He had had nothing to do with the Lisbon earthquake. Nothing, nothing, absolutely nothing. That his only role in the world was to sow. And, even then, he exercised not the slightest control over the fate of the seeds, as his Son had explained in the parable of the Sower. Let him who had eyes to see, see. And ears to hear, hear. And the intelligence to understand, understand. This was what the Great Kyrios told the people of Lisbon that night in the Portuguese supreme court. At the end of which, nervous murmurs and uncontrolled ripples of the throat could be heard. but who would dare contradict the "Governor of Heaven and peoples"? Then, He left. But not before ordering a poisonous flash of light that made a hole in the roof and pulverized the paperwork of the trial. And the judge, trembling, hammered the table so hard that the gavel went flying.

At home, the magistrate received a dressing down so strong that even the angels lay down to see. His women neighbors all boycotted his poor wife and had fled in fear that some greater calamity would manifest itself there. It is not recorded that such misgivings came to pass. To be on the safe side, the judge and the prosecutor, whose wife brandished a razor-sharp pair of scissors, spent the night praying an improvised prayer that demonstrated his fervor: *Misere nobis, Domine, quia minhoca sumus et in minhocam revertemur omnes!* [Have mercy on us, Lord, for we are earthworms and into earthworms are we to turn!] And the Great Kyrios, who traditionally gives everything for a bit of sincere humility, quickly softened with the prayers of hearts toughened and dripping with misfortune. And the two officials, renewed, reconquered the hearts of their wives and recouped the prestige lost with the neighbors. Which once again proved that the Great Kyrios operates with strange methods and along even stranger paths.

Chapter Twenty-Nine

Here the earthworm paused. She coughed again, her throat dry. The shark reacted with another act of gallantry refined from the old times of errant knighthood. He bowed down and scooped some water pooled in the rocks and brought it to her lips. She thanked him with an even greater grace, simultaneously sincere and courtesan-like, while he, visibly enflamed by the proximity, went back to settle close by her, silently debating whether or not he should take the opportunity to give her a quick kiss.

She apologized for having talked at such length, but in reality, the story yet to be told would be even more impressive. She then asked the shark to please relate something of his own origin, his deeds, and the deeds of his people. For she was starting to like the sea and the life there. She felt safe and secure in his company. And if she could, she would leave the mother she so adored, and the perfidious siblings she hated with equal intensity, build a castle overlooking the waves, challenging the winds. With seagulls, beautiful white seagulls hovering, turning, laughing at everything down here and flying away. And she promised to listen to his story with the same eagerness with which he had listened to hers. (A lie of the most refined class of consecrated lies, with dramatic and emotional effect and much utilized nowadays among courting couples.)

The shark honored the request, immediately and gladly, dying to see that moment arrive.

The weather was sublime. . . . (A still bigger lie. He had been badly distracted and at one point had dozed off with a sophisticated snore, much in vogue in the salons, that he had spent time practicing. A certain mocking smile, letting out the thick air in a controlled release from the throat, in such a way that when the snore emerged, he would wake up, open his eyes, smile, greet whoever was in front of him, laughing, uncertain whether he had taken a silent nap or a snoring nap. Except the earthworm was perceptive enough to note the old trick, and diplomatic enough to pretend she hadn't.) He was slack-jawed, delighting in her voice, her manner of description and how she turned the smallest, most mundane things into conversational gems. Therefore, when requested, he did not demur.

Also (the shark began), he had the noble blood of primeval white sharks, kings of the seas, descendants of the Great Tuba, the illustrious paternal grandfather, founder of the hierarchy, feared and respected for his tactics and method of fishing. Who, because of his loves, was nicknamed Tuba-Rei. His lovers, in practice, were all the females in the seas. It was sufficient to draw close and intone to them some sweet nothings that always began with "little girl of my dreams," "little girl of my loves," "little girl of my soul" for them to fall into his arms, sighing from love. Over time, according to the genius of language, the name became modified, and tuba-(rei) was transformed into tuba-(rão), which already appears in the earliest documents of the language without the hyphen, or *tubarão*. There are several philologists, like Zildenstein and Juracyvish, who disagree with that etymology and prefer to base themselves on an apocryphal account, which attributed the origin to the treatment by the lovers of the Great Tuba, who said, "Oh tu, barão, come into my arms!" "Oh tu, barão of my dreams, come make love to me!" Since both etymological versions seem plausible, I leave the choice to whoever wants to choose their own. (Explained the shark.)

He really had a long and penetrating tongue that, placed between his teeth and throat, emitted the strident, concave sound that reverberated over the waters like a battle trumpet. Using that magic tuba, he attracted unwary fishes and invited them to opulent dinners in his underwater mansion. He served them exquisite delicacies. And, after the dinner, after the customary toast of friendship, he would devour them one by one. That granduncle was a multifaceted genius. Besides the tuba, he also imitated the saxophone like a virtuoso. He guffawed, whistled, all that was lacking was for him to speak. He was lord of debate that would be the envy of any democrat trying to make it to the White House. For that very reason, he was called the "Great Gargantua" or "Pantagruel of the seas," nicknames approved by Rabelais.

A legitimate cousin of the female whales who in that epoch divided with them the dominion of the seas. Their bodies began one day to expand and expand, inexplicably, while their interior parts remained the same. So much so that the usual excesses and similar amusements were impossible. Everything went smoothly up to a point, and then... The pudenda shut down, a martyrdom, obviously, besides the embarrassment and the scandal it caused among the cautious fishes, who had condemned any transactions with the whales. The majority, however, talked nonsense and laughed like crazy. The lovers laughed as well, hiding the pain and unwittingly promoting the cruel piling on.

Then, one day the Great Tuba had to undergo major surgery. (Monice's eyes widened in amazement, almost making a face, in a futile effort to seem removed and not understanding. But, just the opposite, feeling pains of suppression, finding the entire matter tragic and hilarious at the same time.) The conclusion was reached that things couldn't continue the way they were. The whales separated from the sharks amicably. It wasn't a divorce en masse in juridical terms, but an amicable separation between them, which did not prevent, one or another, meeting quickly where, delicately but in vain, they sought to avoid the customary drama. Which once more is evidence of the humanistic nature of the shark race. In fact, perceptive psychologists, contradicting anthropology and common sense, affirm that man is merely a primeval shark whose tail split into legs.

In his farewell, the Great Tuba convoked a large gathering, and, emotional and speaking in the name of all, said: "You are our sisters. Choose the seas you like. If you go to the North, we will go to the South. If you choose the East, we will go to the West." And so it has been even today.

However, the females, working only with the gene left to them, with great ability and expertise, developed males of the same species. Which gave rise to the saying: "When a female wants something, sooner or later she'll get it."

We were never again called into service. But there was still a phase when they felt abandoned, mourning our absence and weeping late into the night. They emitted cries more lamented than the sirens of legend. The shark spoke with such arrogance in his voice that he didn't notice the contortions in the visitor's face. He wasn't doing it out of malice but from a superabundance of machismo and dandiness, something extremely common in the species. So common that the saying spread: "Whoever hears the words of a shark should expect to laugh or to vomit."

The whales, however, continued their eternal courtship with poets and psychologists—he continued with resentment—as they had with the prophets, seductive talk in the stories and novels of those times and which continue nowadays.

Chapter Thirty

One Jonah, a with-it hippie, in addition to being a fashionable terrorist by conviction and style, who made no secret of his mortal enmity for the Assyrians, was chosen perforce by the Great Kyrios for a mission among the neighboring peoples. In a bizarre jest of bad taste without parallel in the entire Bible, which would make for a beautiful comic book. Together, revealer and prophet, they unjustifiably falsified the papers of the characters, with the intent of achieving an effect. But what effect did they achieve? To begin with, it had been a granduncle of the Great Tuba, and not a whale, who had housed him for three days. For his heroic action, he was hailed as the "cetacean" [sic!] of the millennium and decorated by the king of Nineveh himself in a formal reception, next to Jonah in a most stirring and moving ceremony. He had swallowed him whole, courteous and chivalrous as etiquette dictates, in order not to ruin the prophet's threadbare clothing. Which, by the way, had a poisonous salty taste from not being washed since he accepted the post as ambassador to Nineveh. And, faithful to his appointment, he hadn't taken a bath for even longer. Bathing had always been considered a rejection of purity and virtue. Which was enough to scramble the brain and turn the stomach of Uncle Tuba, who wandered the seas for three days without knowing where he was or where he was going. He vomited—*Kyrie eleison!* he exclaimed, pumping his fins and looking skyward ecstatically—on the first beach he encountered. That day, he swore never again would he lend his stomach to transport any prophet whoever, even if he were carrying the Ark of the Covenant, not even if the Great Kyrios dumped him at his feet.

The very obvious fact is that even a child could see the absurdity of the prophecy, which from beginning to end seems more like a tall tale than a sacred passage. And if it were true, what kind of Kyrios would transform his message into a joke?

A whale's throat doesn't allow an orange to get through, much less Jonah's feet, even if he had trimmed his toenails. Still, since the beginning of time, whales have enjoyed the attention of prophets, and been heroes of the scribes, who opted to exalt even the cry they uttered. It's not a crying from the eyes but a bellow from the viscera in a furor proportional to the size of the species. A marine defect that plagues them at night for lack of a competent lubricant for the gears. Meanwhile, sharks are held to be barbarians and the villains of the sea, terror of fishermen, bloody butchers hated by all. An unjust reputation, all in all, without merit. Let's look at the statistics. Piranhas, for example, which did deserve such a reputation, never received it. So bloodthirsty and treacherous that the Council of United Fishes expelled them from the seas, they finally found refuge in the heart of the Amazon jungle. (Here, Monice, free of interruption, finally burst out laughing and humming the melody:

> Piranha, piranha
> Let's all piranha
> When it's a piranha day
> You can't mess around . . .

Half-shocked, he gave it little attention, failing to grasp his interlocutor's intention but urging her to continue.)

Shark is a vile, pejorative term nowadays. As we all know. And it has been like that for countless centuries. Nevertheless, we only kill to eat. In our venerable culture, it's an honest way of life, necessary and worthy, and not a sport, to which many men dedicate themselves out of pure laziness, without any need to satisfy hunger or to feed their family. Risking their lives. It was never our intention to make money through our art of fishing. Even now, no one has ever heard of a shark selling fish or human flesh. In a shop installed at water's edge.

Men, on the contrary, daily murder for profit, in addition to cattle and chickens, millions of birds and livestock of every species, not counting the millions of fishes. And not counting the victims of hatred and vengeance they kill and leave to rot on the ground, something inconceivable among our kind. When we disagree with someone, we first employ a diplomatic symbolism, then a tournament of gestures and actions in defense of dignity and constituted rights. And only when all else fails do we resort to bodily confrontation, using warrior arts, with our teeth and everything we have to prove our point of view, or save our honor as king of the sea, defend our rights, establish the inviolable principles granted us by nature. We never use knives, hooks, edged weapons, or the firearms they manufacture. The most powerful nations are not the most cultivated and noble but those that make the most destructive machines. Like the harpoon cannon. Which they shoot into our sides, and drag us bleeding through the seas. I'm not maudlin, and I hate René's whining, who detested the society of men. Each hour among them seemed to open a hole in his chest. *Kyrie eleison!* A hypochondriac like that in a genius work of Christianity! Macedo or even Alencar would never go that far.

Famished wolves give us wild hunting. They replicate the barbaric Achilles, dragging our bleeding body through the waves. A pity no Picasso has so far remembered to leave us a painting worthy of the deed.

They are continually at war, under the pretext of peace, making new wars. and, in order to stay in shape and keep the war industries in full production, they invent small wars here and there. They attack unprepared countries, ragged soldiers, adolescents who aren't even grown, without weapons, Japanese sandals, barefoot, under any pretext that fits the prevailing political agenda, is endorsed by the opposition, and has a pleasant ring in the ears of nations, like "human rights," "universal peace," "the great democracy," "the sacred ecology," "the ten commandments of the rain forest," "hallowed property," "divine capital," "Respect the rodents!" Woe to him who shoots one of them! Or kicks a dog. Recently someone was arrested because he shot a rat behind his house. "An animal who never hurt anyone." There were demonstrations of solidarity and a monument to the rodent was proposed. The mayor supported the cause and saw his popularity skyrocket in the polls. Since the days of Nineveh, no one ever thought of erecting a monument to the shark.

There is never any lack of reasons for a didactic and demonstrative little war. The ecological gentlemen who filled the skies with nuclear explosives and decimated millions decreed that it is savage and inhuman to detonate new bombs. They cut down entire forests from California to Alaska, as it's a crime to touch the trees of the Amazon, "The lung of the world! The lung of the world! Just look!" Well and good, if the Amazon is the lung of the world, and must be maintained in its original state, then Brazil must be compensated for the oxygen produced by the lung of the world. Based on the trillions paid for petroleum that pollutes and kills. You don't need an Einstein to clarify the relationship. In fact, oxygen from the Amazon matters in direct proportion to clean air and in inverse proportion to pollution. The responsible countries should open their eyes and throw the doors wide open for an intelligent and practical discussion of a capital problem of the planet's survival. Today, the king star is our friend, and there is nothing more enjoyable than a sunbath. Humanity will return to dust once he begins to dry up rivers and plant deserts in the forest.

Today's problem is not the hunger of the planet but hunger on the planet. And instead of spending trillions preparing for new wars, we must train people to combat hunger. Man's first obligation is to kill hunger. Damned hunger! Blessed hunger! A thousand times blessed is the empty belly of the famished. It is the engine of work on Earth. In the exchange of mine and thine, that way, this way. In which the clever man takes more and the other man, less. From which progress and riches leap from one hand to the next. And nothing can be done about it. In keeping with the stoical saying of the Messiah. "The poor . . . will always be with you. . . . Let that woman enjoy herself and squander . . ."

The fact is that, as long as hunger lasts on Earth, as long as there are bellies to fill, they will constitute a source of wealth. In the end, it is capital that puts bread on the table and determines who shall and who shall not eat. And who shall not eat anything. Who eats today and who will eat tomorrow. A good capitalist is the one who maintains the balance between buttered bread and an empty belly.

With the harpoon cannon, our life entered a phase of constant threat. In the old day we swept the seas, eating and playing without the least worry. Today, we are on the alert. The smallest motor frightens us, making us feel the hook penetrating our flesh, dragging us through the waters and the jolts of the waves. "Hail, sharks of the earth. We, the sharks of the seas salute you!"

Chapter Thirty-One

Men love a lie. And like a good liar, they make a kyrios of greater proportions. Melville, who in his time was a prophet after his fashion, completely falsified the role of Captain Ahab. Moby Dick dragged him through the waters, made a snack of the old captain. Symbolically, nobly, even ironically as befitted a queen of the seas, all she wanted from him was his heart. As for the rest, she provided a banquet in the seas worthy of the celebrations of earlier times. She tossed his arms and legs into the air. The fishes fell upon them, in noisy delight. The head, which flew into the air, would be the prize for whoever swam the fastest and leapt to grab it before it sank. Even the phlegmatic fishes of Atlantis showed up for the feast. Thanks to the daring Captain Ahab, we had a succulent picnic worthy of remembering. Melville mentions none of this. Captiously, like any narrator of legends. The captain himself, if he were alive, would be the first to belie the nonsense of his gifted prophet. Dignity and character were never lacking in the old sea wolf.

"Hey, come on, come on, how could you, blind as a bat, know nothing but what you heard?" the shark exclaimed dramatically. None of the heroes, no eyewitness who left a single line to substantiate what your lyre sang. And, because he was the first to write down what the people created, he invented a literature similar to that of the *cordel*, the basis of another literature, and gave rise to a famous equation. In the words of the philologists Zildenstein and Juracyvish: Homer is to literature as Moses is to the

Bible.

We are dealing with a people who more than any other on Earth excelled in every genre of prose and poetry. All that epopee is based on the lively imagination of a troubadour who had lost his sight. And, the better the metaphor and the greater the fiction, the more people esteem it and exalt the person telling the lie. One hardly speaks of Aeneas, a hero of the decisiveness of Ulysses, whose snares and cupidity caused him to spend ten years roaming the seas, while the other intrepidly founded the city of seven hills.

According to the account of an old fish (referring to Salmonides, a zealous researcher of history, extremely reliable and balanced in his descriptions, universally recognized as the Herodotus of the seas, whose great feat was revealing the exact location of Atlantis, intact even now with its castles and walls, its temples and homes, its statues, its treasures, the same as when it sank from the horrible separation of the continents. And where Noah's Ark is buried):

The most violent earthquake the planet had ever witnessed, which saw the Americas split to one side, the sisters to the other, and the tragic disappearance of the most beautiful of all. "Farewell, beloved Atlantis, till someday . . ." Like a lovely bride, covered in foam, swallowed up by the giant who adopted her name. "Farewell, Europe! Farewell, America! Farewell, Africa of my heart! Tell the rising sun not to forget—!" sobbed Atlantis, as it was swept under the waves.

Salmonides's descriptions are invaluable for anyone who intends someday to become acquainted with the land now settled at the bottom of the Atlantic and recover the legendary Noah's Ark. He had traveled all the continents, from north to south, from east to west, from the depths of waters to their surface, penetrating rivers like the Nile, the Amazon, the Mississippi. He is said to have left no fewer than 1,500 volumes, histories that predate Jonah, and unpublished episodes of Vasco da Gama, Columbus, and Moby Dick.

The sacking of Troy, as it appears in *The Iliad*, he dared to call "the greatest hoax in verse in recorded history."

In his research, he had discovered that the Trojans strategically burned their own city and slaughtered the Greeks who set foot in it. Those imbeciles in the belly of the horse died of asphyxiation or escaped in the midst of the flames. Ulysses, carried on the backs of his comrades, tremulous, half-dead, his trousers dripping and full. So much for his courage and pride. Paris, the handsomest man in the world, and for that reason also deserving of the most beautiful woman, died a hero, fighting like a wild animal. Helen, sobbing, was filled with remorse and, on her knees, asked for forgiveness before falling into the arms of her husband. An unprecedented folly, unacceptable, in the tradition of Medea and Clytemnestra, for a beautiful woman like Helen. There was no need for such drama. Homer's machismo clearly shows. An absurdity just like the war itself, in its loves, its intrigues, and its motives. The most beautiful woman in the world, according to the testimony of Hera, Venus, and Athena, who acted like gossipy neighbors and envious scandalmongers. Helen had the right to choose the husband she wanted and to change her mind once she chose. By going back to her husband, however, she symbolically removed from Menelaus the most famous horns in History, although invisible in Homer's poem. Obviously, the greatest poet of the times hated the connotation of horns.

Old Priam, in his magnanimity, offered his own daughter,

the prophetess Casandra, to General Agamemnon, in a gesture of peace between the two nations, later cowardly and barbarously betrayed by the irresponsible son of Achilles, who battered the king. His famous myrmidons, in or out of combat, were nothing but true cowards.

In spite of this, Troy recovered and experienced glorious days. (Neither Homer nor anyone else spoke of this.) The envy of Greece, which was lost in fratricidal battles. The real *Iliad* was composed by the Trojan hero and singer Ilíodus, the descendant of a very old and noble family that gave its name to the city Ilia. Homer stole the name, the theme, the style, and completely changed the most brilliant saga of its time. The Greeks, upon learning of the poem and who had composed it, secretly applied a good thrashing to Homer, taking out once and for all his blind eyes. They invaded the city, kidnaped Ilíodus and, after forcing him to sing for the last time, blinded him too, apparently motivated by a legend that blindness made one sing better and purified one's genius (a point about which Salmonides is one hundred percent correct, being that it happened partially to Camões and entirely to Castilho), they cut out his tongue and threw it in a cistern, where every day the prettiest, most talented young women in Greece would descend, seeking to reproduce in themselves his genius, with Greek and Trojan blood. He was a simple man, but of gigantic stature and predicates. Some patriots, dreamers and inventive, brought him young, fiery mares, from which the centaurs are said to have originated. They feared, however, that Ilíodus would become a divinity too large to exclude from Hellenic glories. Therefore, his name must be completely expunged from the memory of men. Troy, destroyed, likewise would have forgotten him. Only much later, his figure reappeared among the lost notes of Aeneas. However, says Salmonides, it was from these preambles and circumstances that emerged the geniuses of the greatest civilization on Earth, and the famous Golden Age of Greece.

It was in the interest of the Greeks for the fame of Homer to spread and for his epic work to be covered with glory. Ilíodus, already old, resentful, but still lively in spirit, wrote some verses that translated his pain and are reminiscent of Virgil:

> *Hos ego versiculos feci*
> *Tullit alter honores*
> *Sic vos non vobis nidificatis aves*
> *Sic vos non vobis vellera fertis oves*
> *Sic vos non vobis mellificatis apes*
> *Sic vos non vobis fertis aratra boves*

[I wrote these verses. / Another garnered the honors. / Thus, you do not make nests for yourselves, birds. / Thus, you do not produce wool for yourselves, sheep. / Thus, you do not make honey for yourselves, bees. / Thus, you do not pull plows for yourselves, oxen.]

Chapter Thirty-Two

That business of writers and poets making up things as they like comes from bygone times. Using metaphors, they created worlds they filled with angels, demons, and similar beings. They planted heavens. They founded hells. Stories like those you told, all fabrications of genius creators, the human cultural heritage, that we received from the woman called Eve. Here, a man of clay, a woman from a rib, a poisoned apple, a crime punished endlessly over the centuries. There, a centaur, a faun, an army crossing the sea on foot yet staying dry, a giant who brought down the columns of a temple; a nymph, a mermaid, a virgin who remains a virgin before and after giving birth. All because of a child in a basket, floating on the current.

Thus appears Moses, disputing with Homer, the greatest of all, or his neighbor. Then, Virgil vying with Dante for the position of runner-up. After them, the unending line of pinkies and index fingers. To a man, all dedicated to the fabrication of metaphors. And with those metaphors they created the myth and the world in which we live.

Moses and Homer, however, were students from the same school of metaphors and myths, with the world's oldest located on the banks of the Euphrates, ever since man invented speech and forged the art of words. With all the enchantment it creates. Rhythm, melody, the chorus, riding the metaphor and spreading the image of the myth.

One day Homer said, "Look, Moses, there are already enough

myths for a forest of books." Moses, less dour that day, agreed: "You're right, Homer, let's bring everything together and make it just one story. I'll tell it one way, you, another, and in the end, we'll choose which is prettier."

"Fine," said Homer. "Let's get to work!" They sat down at their desks, each with a jug of wine, their loaf of bread, and candles to allow working at night. Soon, mosquitoes appeared, and they began arguing differences in method, style, and content. Whether to use verse or prose. To sing or recite. With the help of a chorus or without. The greatest disagreement was the number of kyrioses, whether one, or many at the same time. The fights the kyrioses had for only one of them to take power and command over the others. Whether the rule would be democratic or absolute. Whether they had the vices and virtues of their subjects, or only virtues and no vices. A deadly war among vassals. Whether the Kyrioses had created men, or men had created the Kyrioses. Finally, whether man came from woman or woman from man.

They were unable to arrive at an agreement. Homer, hot and tired, emptied his jug on Moses's head. To retaliate, Moses stuck a candle in Homer's eye. Afterwards, they came to their senses and sheepishly shook hands, returning to their respective countries for further study of the superstitions of their people and the adages of the prophets. And thus it was that the two greatest sagas in human history came about.

Homer, already blind, settled for recounting in heroic verses what he had heard from troubadours and poets since childhood in the streets, the declamations in the squares, the songs accompanied by lyre, narrating the origin of the kyrioses of Olympus, the nights of storms catching fire between the clouds, grand narratives in prose and verse transmitted from father to son, the fights for power, all of it a brilliant reflection of the human soul, producing the greatest epopee of all time.

Moses, dramatic, appears as narrator, but much more imaginative in creating what would be an epic in prose, Genesis and Exodus, fearless and abounding with eschatological vision. In keeping with rules and style, brilliant in the practice and the game or politics, it went much further, creating the history of the world to meet the desire of his people, in a way that no one had yet conceived, in which he became prophet, leader, and messiah of the very Kyrios who emerged from his pen. In that sense, the Pentateuch appears, a beautiful messianic saga, the best of its kind. In Homer, the people create the great kyrioses of Olympus and use them when the occasion arises of one needing the other. In Moses, the Great Kyrios creates the world and, in it, his chosen people. But both were right. The form, the style, the content doesn't matter. What would be a world without Kyrios, democratic or absolute, to fill the emptiness in the soul, the abysses of the mind? What would become of the palaces, the squares, the temples, the Sistine chapels? Of literature and art, in short?

Salmonides doesn't hide his preference for Homer and his serious misgivings about Moses. According to him, that saga about plagues in Egypt is not mentioned in any archive of the seas, or the rivers of that period. In fact, the plagues of Egypt are a grave insult to the Creator of mankind, the heavens, the seas, and the very people of Israel for whom Moses wrote the epic of the Exodus. The plagues make the Great Kyrios into a sorcerer inferior to Shakespeare's witches, or like Goethe's Mephisto. There, the Lord of Lords and angelic hosts, the Governor of Heaven and peoples struggles as he tries to persuade a simple Egyptian king, no mental or physical giant, which he could accomplish with a mere gesture, a mere desire, a well-placed rap on the head with the knuckles, a kick in the butt.

With his command of metaphors, Moses parted the waters of the Red Sea so the Jews could pass through without getting their feet wet and closed to engulf the Pharaoh's infantry and horsemen. Now, that would have been the most fabulous banquet-at-sea in History, greater than Melville's Captain Ahab, and would have entered the memory of fishes, even the vegetarians and the phlegmatic completely uninterested in marine gossip.

My grandparents always laughed when they heard that fable. The sharks of those waters, even if they never heard of Salmonides, repeat what every fish dies knowing, that he has no idea what the flesh of an Egyptian horse tastes like. Now, if the Great Kyrios really wanted to get the Jews out of trouble, he wouldn't need such farfetched tactics. All of which were clichés for the benefit of the pharaoh's court magicians, who reported each of the plagues faithfully, without attributing them to any specific Kyrios or claiming for themselves anything other than the privileges of sorcerers. It seems, in fact, blasphemous to think that a Great Kyrios, admired and feared, would need plagues to persuade a mortal. Without achieving the desired effect. With these episodes, Moses wrote the Exodus, while Homer wrote *The Odyssey*.

Why take the Red Sea when they could cross Suez with dry feet? Naturally, the spectacle and the triumph of the waters were the great motivation. Salmonides says that Homer (who never stopped corresponding with his schoolmate) wrote a letter to Moses congratulating him in general terms but mocking the ending. He emphasized that, where Ulysses returned and took revenge against his enemies, Moses got lost in the desert without seeing the promised land. From all indications, he died without having read the letter, nor do we know if he would have replied.

Getting back to the Pharaoh, Salmonides says, after all, he was just doing his civil duty. Promoting the well-being of the people and the country's economy. Now, freeing labor was the same as freeing the slaves, which has always resulted in wars around the world. Did the slaves in Greece or Rome, or in Solomon's court, ever consider going to their masters to say that the Kyrios they worshiped was ordering them to bundle up their stuff and leave? And that they, Lords and Kings, had better obey and let them go, lest they incur his wrath and see plagues inflict the entire country?

We mustn't crucify the poets and narrators. Nor throw stones at guitar players and street versifiers with their power of rhyme and the magic of words. They merely wrote down on paper the best fables of their time. For the glory of their nation, the amusement of people, and, above all, the dream of immortality hidden in every verse, in every line, in every melody. In this way Homer, Moses, Virgil, and Dante, Cervantes, Verdi, Bizet, Beethoven, Strauss, and Shakespeare still live.

One further point of contrast. Homer speaks of the kyrioses of Olympus but leaves everything as he found it, while Moses put himself at the center of all he created. He enters History in a basket bobbing lost on the waters of the Nile, is taken to Pharaoh's court, but attempts to destroy the king who adopted him as a son. Which would make him a monster of ingratitude, unworthy of the role of hero, much less of messiah. Wouldn't it have been much easier to force the political integration of the Jews, impose human rights, and Israel, with its dynamism, its spirit of struggle, its perspicacious vision of everything, which produced an Elias, a David, a Solomon, a Joseph, a Jesus Christ, a Freud, an Einstein, who knows if they would have ended up inheriting the throne of Egypt?

Didn't Constantine, the son of a boardinghouse maid, inherit all of the Roman empire? At least the Jews could claim descent from the viceroy, who had saved the country from poverty and hunger. In any case, wouldn't it be simpler and more practical than to set out randomly into the world in search of the unknown land, killing, spilling the blood of and expelling the people they encountered on the way, all in the name of a Kyrios, Father of all, the poor and the rich indiscriminately? A Kyrios whom they themselves neither recognized or feared, given that, after everything, after the plagues, the death of the Egyptians' first-born, the crossing of the Red Sea, the manna in the desert, the Israelites thought little of it and, holding Moses to be a cheap charlatan, came up with the idea of making a golden calf that they worshiped and believed would deliver them from the desert. Now, that is an insult to the pen of Moses and the intelligence of the Hebrew people. No one would have the courage to confront the ire of the Great Kyrios after so many proofs of his power in his presence. No Greek, or even Roman, however audacious or stupid, would have the impudence to make Jupiter into an idiot, not to mention the anger of Athena, if, instead of worshiping him, they worshiped a goat in the square. The Kyrioses, jealous and vindictive by nature, would not tolerate such insults.

And Salmonides continued:

Moses, however, is a writer of prose, and prose so perfect that it turned into prophecy everything that emerged from his pen. Fantastic Moses! Rival of Homer, who ceded to his colleague the title of emperor of Literature and assumed for himself the crown of Judaism.

I disagree with Xenophanes when he says that "all of that is only a web of suppositions," when he should say that all of it is only an epopee of metaphors. With metaphors, really, worlds are created, religions and empires are founded, populated by saints, demons and prophets, and even a Messiah born of a virgin, without human intervention, who shakes the world like the most sublime of metaphors. He, the poor Messiah in the role he assumed, like Moses, would fail in his mission as leader of his people, condemned by his own, betrayed by a brother, and ended up as a rogue on a cross. It was his role as hero in the drama of the apple. With his blood he would redeem the world. Without the luck and abilities of Theseus, who skillfully killed the minotaur, he in fact died in vain. He didn't redeem the metaphor, and the world still awaits his return, or another Messiah to appear in his stead.

All these stories involved human awareness of an action and form, which becomes almost impossible for man, today, to escape. Blame Homer and Moses. All the animals on Earth, no less the fishes in the entire world, pity men. Ah, the miserable human soul, besieged by millions of monsters and goblins, where is your Ariadne? Where does the Theseus hide who will free you from the labyrinth of myths?

The shark again referred to his cousins the dolphins, for whom he barely disguises his resentment, envy, and admiration at the same time. "The favorite of children and grownups . . . who'll give anything for a show and die for applause. They live as if life were a circus with clowns as the only act."

Chapter Thirty-Three

Here, Clyto the shark paused and gave a deep sigh. Monice, hitherto rapt and absorbed, distantly meditating, suddenly drew back and laughed slightly. Then she said:

"Look, forgive me for interrupting . . . but when you spoke about dolphins and applause, suddenly I found myself on the runway, seems that I was dreaming . . ."

"My Queen of Beauty . . . come and dream in my arms . . . I am, beyond any doubt, the handsomest of all sharks in the seas . . ." (He put on a laughing face, showing his teeth and inflating his chest in a customary pose.) "A small walk on the beach wouldn't hurt, right, my little girl?"

She looked to the side, feigning total indifference. Feigning boredom. Finally, she added:

"So . . . you must have a lot of fun . . . and you don't lack for girlfriends, yes?"

Surprised by the question, he gulped and managed to say:

"Well . . . One, two, maybe three . . . no one like you . . . so different . . . so pink and tender . . . your air of a doll, your skin like a poppy . . . I swear by the soul of Moby Dick there's nothing in the world compares to you . . . enchanting little girl . . . a dream of an earthworm . . . there truly isn't, no . . ."

He was sincere. His entire soul bubbled up on his lips. The whole of his being burned with desire to possess the little thing, right there, in that instant. But she, still ironically, said:

"Stop it . . . you, the declared enemy of metaphors!" she said, again feigning indifference. Affecting distance. Afterwards, sensing the vacuum growing and that he was not reacting:

"Those beaches, tell me about those picturesque beaches..."

"Ah!... close, just a short way, really nothing... the warm water... divine... there's nothing better than lazing on the white sand of the beach..."

The earthworm could no longer answer, entranced by his presence and the way he looked. His strength, his vigor. Her face burned every time he spoke, that deep voice in his chest, vibrating inside her. Tremulous, not knowing how to act. How to control herself. He approached, as if to kiss her, take her under his power. In a rapture, she already felt herself being possessed. She knew that even if she wanted to, she couldn't resist. He... so large... so powerful... penetrating with softness and tenderness.... Then, her mind clouded. She regretted that she was still a virgin. "Good heavens! Woe is me!" Her throat knotted up, anticipating rejection. What would he do when he realized it? Then!... She had heard of cases. Dramas. Acts of madness. Suicides. She remembered how Diolito had cursed her bitterly. Her hesitation and manners. "The devil!... what indolence!"

She had never felt like this. What was it in her that he was so attracted to? A simple earthworm far from the things of life. He, so large, so imposing, dominating the waves that curved at his feet. An unsolicited desire came to her. Ah, if only she had wings! She would love to have wings and fly like the seagulls over the waves, with him running behind, following her. "Come down, come down, my beloved little girl!" and fall into his arms, rolling with him... in the warm shallows of the shore. "Ah! delirious! Ah! darling! Sweet passion!"

At that exact instant, like a hurricane in the waters, a motor launch growled from behind the rocks and a voice exclaimed, "What a lovely earthworm!"

The shark quickly bolted, and the hapless earthworm, impaled on the hook, thrashed in the wind.

THE END

Ave Canis: A Rare Interview with Domício Coutinho
July 31, 2022

George Salis: You published a novel in 1998 titled *Duke, the Dog Priest*, which was translated from the Portuguese by Clifford E. Landers and brought out by Green Integer in 2009. Other than this masterwork, have you written any novels since then?

Domício Coutinho: Yes, in Portuguese. The title of which is: *Incríveis Revelações de uma Minhoca*. It was never translated and a good translation into English would be: "*Revelations of a Water Bait* [or *Earthworm*]." Published in Brazil in 2000 [Recife Ed. Bagação].

GS: What can you tell English readers about *Incríveis Revelações de uma Minhoca*? What are we missing out on?

DC: This novel is an allegorical one with what one may say are certain 18th-century, Voltaire-like aspects. Modesty prevents me from revealing more, except to say that I long for the day that it will be translated into English.

GS: Was *Duke, the Dog Priest* your first novel, or did you have earlier projects you worked on that were not published?

DC: It was my first novel.

GS: It seems *Duke, the Dog Priest* was written quite later in your life, perhaps in your 60s or 70s? Do you think writing a novel like this was easier with the experience and wisdom of that age range or do you wish you had started it sooner?

DC: Yours is a difficult question to answer. Especially as I do not adhere to Said's concept of the "late style" in art. Obviously, when one has accumulated x number of years of existence, that tends to be reflected in one's artistic work. Enough said.

GS: How would you describe your awakening as a writer?

DC: The sudden illumination of/in your mind of a common, everyday event which sticks out in your mind, and it absorbs your entire attention and from which a work of fiction emerges. That seems to be a very common occurrence among writers of fiction, I believe.

GS: You earned a bachelor's degree in Aristotelian Thomistic theology from the Gregorian University of Rome. What was that educational experience like and did it influence the theological themes in your novel?

DC: Well, the point of Thomistic theology is that it creates the basis for rational thinking, cause and effect, of natural philosophy. Cause and effect of all things. Due to the fact that nature is an open book for everyone to read and learn and to draw their own conclusions. So it adjusts your life accordingly.

GS: Among other things, *Duke, the Dog Priest* is delightfully irreverent when it comes to religion. What would you say to someone who would accuse you of blasphemy? Is no topic off-limits in the world of art?

DC: This is a blind reaction to someone who comes to express themselves irreverently. My novel is a satire against celibacy. It shows that celibacy is in contradiction to the Divine Maker's original divine instruction: "to grow and multiply." Catholic doctrine in this instance is contrary to God's command in this instance. They are blaspheming, not I.

GS: In 2006, you founded The Brazilian Library of New York, which houses thousands of books. Perhaps this is an impossible question, but I'd like to know what five titles you would choose for a miniature version of The Brazilian Library?

DC: That is a very good question! I would say something from Machado de Assis (the most Europeans of Brazilian writers); José de Alencar; Luís de Camões Castro Alves; Gonçalves Dias.

[In a brief and undated video interview about his unique library, Coutinho emphasized, "Libraries are the most visible and noble symbols of a people's culture."]

GS: What's a novel you've read and think deserves more readers?

DC: José de Alencar's *Iracema*. The mythos of "Brazilianism" is reflected in this splendid work. The unification of the sophisticated European male with the "creature of nature," female, is shown to result in the mixture that is a Brazilian.

GS: João Guimarães Rosa's *Grande Sertão: Veredas* (translated into English by James L. Taylor and Harriet de Onís under the title *The Devil to Pay in the Backlands*) is often hailed as the Brazilian *Ulysses*. Have you read it? What would you consider the Brazilian counterpoint of James Joyce's *Ulysses* if not Rosa's novel?

DC: Yes, I have read it, greatly enjoyed it, and consider it the Brazilian equivalent of Joyce's modernist masterpiece. What more does one have to say? For me that is enough to label it superb.

GS: What are your fondest memories of growing up in Brazil?

DC: It is the tradition of the celebration of the Saint John the Baptist's name day in late June of each year. Dancing and singing all night around a bonfire. A uniquely Brazilian event.

GS: What was your motivation for emigrating to New York in 1959? Was it difficult acclimating to this new environment? Was there any culture shock?

DC: My coming to New York was accidental: I met a beautiful Austrian girl in 1956, just as I was deciding to quit the seminary to become a priest. I became involved with her and we became engaged. But, I had to go back to Brazil and decided to go to law school to acquire knowledge sufficient for a legal career. At the same time, I took a degree in Anglo-German literature. We corresponded via mail. She was very romantic and sent me many pictures and poems. Even a lock of her hair. And to fulfill my promise to visit her, and on the way to Vienna, I stopped off in New York. There was at the time no direct flights from Brazil to Austria. I had to stay overnight in New York. However, that particular night, I went to mass as it was a Sunday and was anxious to take communion from Bishop Fulton Sheen, who I met in Roma. Which required that I confess and for sake of fluency, I confessed in Latin. And the priest hearing the confession was so impressed with my Latin, that he offered me a job as a sacristan on the spot. $45.00 a week. The minimum salary then. And that caused me to stay. No cultural shock. I was in love with New York and having lived for more than three years in Roma and having traveled all over Europe, acclimatizing was relatively easy.

[When Coutinho was honored by the Câmara do Recife in 2004, he said, "Only a Brazilian who is far from the country can appreciate the importance of his own nation. [...] I carry Pernambuco with me in my heart, because I am from Paraíba by origin, but from Pernambuco by adoption. [...] . . . every Brazilian, when he takes the first step outside the country, necessarily becomes a kind of ambassador, because he is representing his homeland." (Translated from the Portuguese.)]

GS: Near the beginning of your novel, it is written that "Inside every dog dwells a silent man, and inside every man dwells a barking dog." What is your dog barking about?

DC: My dog barks inside my head all the time: about natural philosophy, cause and effect. What is and what is not the beginning of the cause of other things. The nature & lessons of mother nature.

GS: What would you say if you were in the confessional with Duke, the dog priest?

DC: A personal sin that I might have committed recently.

GS: As someone who has championed the arts for many decades, do you have hope for the future of literature and art in general?

DC: Yes, absolutely, because the nature of the arts and literature is to describe the beauty of nature and most of all the beauty of human beings, the masterwork of nature.

About the Author

Born in João Pessoa, Brazil in 1931, Domício Coutinho emigrated to the United States in 1959, eventually earning a Master's and Ph.D. in Comparative Literature from the City University of New York (CUNY) in addition to his bachelor's degree in Aristotelian Thomistic theology from the Gregorian University of Rome. In 1986, Coutinho, with his wife and two sons, began a business in real estate appropriation and management of properties. In 1999, Coutinho founded The Brazilian Writers Association of New York (UBENY). In 2002, he was admitted as Commander into the Order of Rio Branco, a Brazilian Institution honoring those who have distinguished themselves in cultural and patriotic achievements. In 2004, Coutinho founded the Brazilian Endowment for the Arts (BEA), a non-profit organization dedicated to preserving and promoting the Brazilian Arts, Literature, and Cultural Traditions for the Brazilian/American and Latin American Communities. That same year, he created The Machado de Assis Medal of Merit to honor those who distinguish themselves in Brazilian Cultural Traditions. In 2006, Coutinho founded The Brazilian Library of New York, which houses 7,000 titles, with an auditorium for events, conferences, literary gatherings, films, and dramatic performances. The library has been visited by prominent representatives from government, diplomacy, and academia.

Aside from an untranslated poetry collection titled *Salomônica* (1975) and the novel titled *Incredible Revelations of an Earthworm*, Coutinho published a novel in 1998 titled *Duke, the Dog Priest*, which was translated from the Portuguese by Clifford E. Landers and brought out by Green Integer in 2009.

Acknowledgments

Thanks to the following for their generous financial support which helped to defray some of this publication's production costs:

Thomas Young Barmore Jr, Sam Bertram, Brian R. Boisvert, BON COMICS, Tobias Carroll, Celestine de la Tour, Scott Chiddister, Greg Cobb, Eric L. Collette, Joshua Lee Cooper, Parker & Malcolm Curtis, Robert Dallas, James Duncan, Andrew Eagle, Echo, Isaac Ehrlich, Dayna Epley, Robert Farwell, Ken Finlayson, Michael Denley Fischer, E Gaustad, GMarkC, Jason Gray, Everett Haagsma, Aric Herzog, Dave Holets, Sam 5210 Horn, Conor Hultman, Fred W Johnson, Jacob H Joseph, Stefan Kruger, Leonore the Wanderer, Jim McElroy, Donald McGowan, Ian McMillan, Jody Mock, Steven Moore, Jhon Mor, Geoffrey Moses, Gregory Moses, Scott Murphy, Erga Netz, Richard Novak, Matt O'Connell, Michael O'Shaughnessy, Sheri Jean Olsen-Skillin, Andrew Pearson, Vladimir Poleganov, Pedro Ponce, Quintin, Judith Redding, Owen Rowe, Florian Schiffmann, Seda, K. Seifried, Dillon Sim, Robert E. Slaven, K. L. Stokes, Stephen Tabler, Dan Theodore, Evan Wagoner, Chee Lup Wan, Christopher Wheeling, Isaiah Whisner, Charles Wilkins, T.R. Wolfe, and the The Zemenides Family

www.ingramcontent.com/pod-product-compliance
Lightning Source LLC
LaVergne TN
LVHW031606060526
838201LV00063B/4752